Eye of the HURRICANE

Lee Roddy

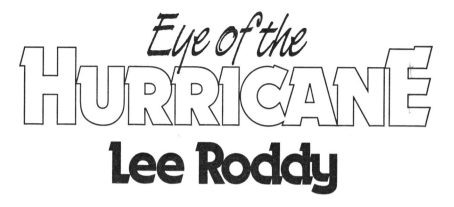

PUBLISHING

Colorado Springs, Colorado

EYE OF THE HURRICANE
Copyright © 1994 by Lee Roddy
All rights reserved. International copyright secured.

Library of Congress Cataloging-in-Publicaton Data applied for.

Roddy, Lee, 1921—
    Eye of the hurricand / Lee Roddy.
        p.   cm. — (Ladd family adventure series)
    Summary: A petty quarrel and efforts to foil poachers who are after some rare birds
seem unimportant as members of the Ladd family separately struggle to survive when a
powerful hurricane hits the island of Kauai.
    ISBN 1-56179-220-9
    [1. Hurricanes—Fiction.   2. Hawaii—Fiction.   3. Brothers and sisters—Fiction.
4. Christian life—Fiction.]   I. Title.   II. Series: Roddy, Lee, 1921— Ladd family
adventure.
    PZ7.R6Ey   1994
    [Fic]—dc20
                                                                                94-11781
                                                                                     CIP
                                                                                      AC

Published by Focus on the Family Publishing,
Colorado Springs, Colorado 80995
Distributed by Word Books, Dallas, Texas.

The author is represented by the literary agency of Alive Communications, P.O. Box 49068,
Colorado Springs, CO 80920

This is a work of fiction, and any resemblance between the characters in this book and real
persons is coincidental.

Editor: Ron Klug
Cover Illustration: Paul Casale
Cover Designer: James Lebbad

Printed in the United States of America
94 95 96 97 98 99/10 9 8 7 6 5 4 3 2

Dedicated to
Phil and Lynn Luttrell
and their children,
Joshua, Jonathan, Benjamin, and Rebecca
of Kauai Christian Academy.

ACKNOWLEDGMENTS

The author wishes to express his appreciation to all those who shared their experiences as survivors of Hurricane Iniki or contributed research that acted as a springboard for this novel.

The characters are totally fictitious, but the author tried hard to accurately portray the hurricane, while taking some literary license in places and events to produce a stronger story.

Special thanks goes to Mary Daubert of *The Kauai Times;* Sky Fischer of Akahi Farm, Haiku, Maui; Christopher Mandeville of Kilauea, Kauai; Tom Telfer, district wildlife biologist, State Division of Forestry and Wildlife and Department of Land and Natural Resources, Lihue, Kauai; Eugene Erskine, president of Papillon Helicopters, Honolulu; and the Luttrell family of Lihue.

A special *mahalo* goes to Phil and Lynn Luttrell of Kauai Christian Academy and their children, Joshua, 12; Jonathan, 9; Benjamin, 5; and baby Rebecca. Lynn provided invaluable assistance in several areas, for which the author is most grateful.

CONTENTS

Chapter One

THE THREAT OF COMING STORM

Josh Ladd suddenly awakened and jerked upright on his beach air mattress. The top sheet dropped away with the waterproof tarp he'd used in case it drizzled.

He had been uncomfortably dreaming about the argument he'd had yesterday with Tiffany. It wasn't just a brother-and-sister disagreement, but had been mean-spirited, with Tiffany screaming angrily at him.

Yet that wasn't what awakened him. Rather, it was a sound that seemed out of place at dawn of Friday, September 11 on the island of Kauai's* Na Pali* Coast. The trade winds had died down. The air was very humid.

Tank Catlett, Josh's best friend, raised his head from where he slept a few feet away. "What're you doing?"

Josh glanced seaward and saw a white helicopter with brilliant arched colors flying unusually low about a hundred yards off shore. "I wonder what one of those sight-seeing Rainbow Helicopters is doing out so early?"

Suddenly, the aircraft banked sharply and headed low and

straight toward the boys. The pilot was clearly visible behind the plexiglass. He slowed and started settling on the beach.

"Something's wrong," Josh decided, pulling on his cutoff blue jeans under the sheet. "Oh, I hope it's not bad news about my dad!" He struggled into his red aloha* shirt and stood up. He ran barefooted toward the aircraft as its skids touched the earth.

Tank also hurriedly dressed in blue cutoffs and a white tee shirt. Barefooted, with uncombed blond hair, he joined Josh as the pilot opened the right-hand door.

He jumped out while the overheard rotor still turned slowly. He wore tennis shoes, tan shorts, and a white short-sleeved shirt with gold epaulets on the shoulders.

"You two alone?" he asked as the boys approached. As they silently nodded, he ordered, "Okay, get aboard. There's a hurricane coming."

"Hurricane?" Josh cried in disbelief, looking at the clear, beautiful dawn sky. "Yesterday the weather reports said it was going to miss Hawaii."

"It changed direction," the pilot replied, turning and hurrying toward the chopper. "It's going to hit this island dead center about noon today!"

"Uh . . ." Josh said, stopping so suddenly his bare feet sank into the sandy beach. "We can't go! My father and his friend are walking out of Alakai Swamp* this morning. We're here to meet them."

"Get aboard," the pilot said crisply. "We'll fly inland and try to find them."

"Thanks!" Josh replied. "We'll get our camping . . ."

"Leave your gear!" the pilot interrupted. "There's no time. Just grab your shoes and get aboard."

Josh ran back, snatched up his and Tank's tennis shoes, then scrambled aboard the French-made helicopter. There was room for six passengers, but there was no one aboard except the boys and the pilot.

He sat on the right in front and motioned for Josh to sit next to him and for Tank to take the left seat. The boys had flown in helicopters before, so they automatically fastened their seat belts and adjusted their headsets.

To be heard above the engine's noise, the pilot spoke into his microphone. "The fire department asked us to make a search for hikers. You boys are the first ones I've seen. We'll try to find your two men and get them aboard. That'll still give us room for a couple more people if we can locate them. Then we'll fly to safety."

Twelve-year-old Josh brushed his wavy brown hair away from his blue eyes as the aircraft rose rapidly. He noticed that an unusually high surf pounded the coast. The sky was clear, without a single cloud.

The helicopter cleared the tops of the steep cliffs, then leveled out over a breathtaking valley. It was one of countless lush verdant spots resplendent with trees and flowering bushes. Such beauty had earned Kauai its designation as the Garden Isle.

Beyond the series of peaks and countless waterfalls near rainy Mount Waialeale* lay remote, desolate Alakai Swamp.

Very few people ever dared venture there, but three days before, Josh's father and Daniel Nakamura, an ornithologist* friend, had hiked into the swamp.

Dr. Nakamura claimed to have found a pair of colorful and exotic Kauai 'o'o'a'a* birds thought to be extinct. He had shown the family a map indicating where he had seen the birds. He had then taken Mr. Ladd, publisher of a Hawaiian tourist newspaper, to break the news to the public.

There had been great secrecy about the mission because Dr. Nakamura, a family friend, had confided to them that other rare birds from around the world were known to be worth up to $100,000 each.

A nesting pair of presumed extinct Hawaiian birds could be priceless. So poachers must not be allowed to learn of the 'o'o habitat.

Josh anxiously peered down, hoping to see his father and Dr. Nakamura hiking on the trail below.

"There!" the pilot exclaimed. "I see two men below."

The helicopter had rounded a corner and was already settling onto a small open meadow within a hundred yards of two men on the trail.

Josh raised his voice again. "That's not my father or his friend."

"Well, whoever they are," the pilot said as the chopper's skids touched down, "we're going to keep them from trying to survive a hurricane in the open."

Moments later the pilot opened the right door and hurriedly explained to the two strangers about the coming hurricane.

Both men had backpacks, hiking boots and light yellow rain gear. A piece of burlap sack showed in the pocket of the rain jacket carried by the taller, dark-complexioned man.

The pilot concluded, "So leave your camping gear and get aboard quickly, please."

The big man protested. "We can't leave our tent and all the rest of our camping supplies. They cost plenty."

"Sorry, but there's no choice," the pilot said. "With the load of fuel I'm carrying, and knowing we're planning to pick up another two grown men, we can't risk any extra weight."

"Look, mister . . . ," tall man began.

"Keegan," the pilot interrupted. "I'm Jerry Keegan."

"I'm Chester Franks," the big man replied. "He's Sylvester Garcia. Who are the kids?"

"I'm Josh Ladd," the boy said. "This is Tank Catlett."

Both Franks and Garcia ignored the boys' extended right hands. Josh felt an instant distaste for the men, who removed their backpacks and threw them aboard, followed by their rain gear. Several papers slid out of the pocket of Franks' raincoat. With an oath, he hastily recovered them from under the middle seat, then climbed aboard, followed by Garcia.

The pilot said crisply, "Take the middle or back seats, please. Get your seat belts and headsets on."

Franks asked, "Why can't we sit in front where those kids are?"

"A little thing called C.G.," Keegan explained. "That means center of gravity. Hurry, please. As soon as we're airborne, I'll radio home base and give them your names, with the names of the two men we're looking for."

Garcia, the shorter man, had an unusually long neck, giving him a turtle-like appearance. He didn't say much although his companion muttered under his breath. Both settled in the rear seats.

As the helicopter lifted off, Josh saw Tank looking at him. The blond boy gave a slight jerk of his head toward the rear seat. Tank rolled his eyes upward in a sign of disgust.

They're lucky to be alive, Josh thought. *Now let's hope we find Dad and his friend fast.*

The pilot sent the chopper scooting skyward, then leveled out. The taller stranger leaned toward the pilot and tapped him on the shoulder. "Hey, Keegan," Franks said loudly to be heard above the engine's noise, "my friend and I have to get back to Princeville* in a hurry. Take us there now, and we'll make it worth your while."

The pilot spoke into his microphone. "I'm not making this trip for money. People will die down there if we don't find them before that hurricane hits."

Franks spoke more forcefully, "Listen, Keegan, this storm won't get here for another few hours. That's plenty of time for you to drop us off at Princeville and then come back to continue your search."

"Sorry, I can't do that," the pilot replied, shifting hands on the stick with its various control buttons. "The window of opportunity for flying is a lot less than five hours. Those two men down there won't have a chance if we don't find them pretty soon and get out before the first winds make it unsafe to fly."

"What's so important about them?" Franks demanded.

Josh stiffened, but before he could say anything, the pilot explained. "Well, for one thing, they're human beings." His voice was suddenly cool. "And this boy sitting next to me might not have a father if we don't find them in time."

Josh was angered at the tall man's attitude, but he kept his voice calm as he tried to explain. "My dad and his friend, Dr. Nakamura, are hiking back from the swamp. Tank and I were going to meet them when they walked out this morning."

Josh saw the two strangers exchange meaningful looks. Franks asked, "Did you say Dr. Nakamura?"

Josh nodded. "Dr. Daniel Nakamura is an ornith . . ." Josh let his words trail off as the two men again looked at each other.

When the shorter man nodded, Franks turned toward the pilot. "Uh, maybe I was a bit hasty, Mr. Keegan." With a sudden smile that Josh thought was not sincere, the man continued. "Garcia and I will naturally put aside our pressing concerns in hopes you'll locate the boy's father and Dr. Nakamura. We'll help you look."

Josh was relieved but puzzled at the men's sudden change of attitude. He pondered this as the pilot asked the passengers for phone numbers where home base could notify someone about who was aboard and where they were going. Josh and Tank gave the Nakamura number, but the two men said they didn't need to notify anyone.

That's strange, Josh mused. *Why wouldn't they want somebody to know where they were?*

Josh shrugged and turned his attention again to searching the ground below. He desperately wanted to see his father striding along on his long legs, but nobody was in sight.

Keegan announced, "We've got to climb above one more mountain peak. When we drop down on the other side, we'll be leaving the valley and entering the swamp. There are not many places to land down there, so when we see those two men, we may have to hover and help them aboard."

Josh nodded and turned to Tank. His hair, bleached almost white from the sun, was uncombed above his nose, which was always sunburned and peeling. Like Josh, his arms and shoulders were well developed from a lifetime of swimming.

The helicopter climbed steeply, rising above the peak, giving Josh and the others a brief overall glimpse of the Alakai Swamp spread out before them.

From his father's talk before leaving on his expedition with Nakamura, Josh knew that the Alakai was not really a swamp. Rather, it was the last remnants of a tropical rain forest now designated as a wilderness preserve. It rests around the 4000- to 5000-foot elevation, and is forested with a few boggy areas.

The area is tropical, with many mosses and ferns. It is very lush, with virtually all native plants and birds, some of which are found nowhere else on earth.

The helicopter's plexiglass nose suddenly pointed downward, starting a steep descent. Josh's stomach seemed to squeeze up into his throat.

The pilot announced with a chuckle, "I usually play classical tunes on these trips, matching the rise and fall of the music with the aircraft. I've got a dandy for this one going down, but you'll all have to imagine it."

As the chopper continued its sharp downward slant, Josh felt something brush against his bare feet. He glanced down at a piece of folded paper. He absently picked it up, thinking some previous passenger must have dropped it.

As the helicopter completed its steep descent and leveled out about 50 feet above the ground, Josh opened the paper. He glanced at it and blinked in surprise.

That's Dr. Nakamura's map to the birds' area! But how did it get in here?

His thoughts were snapped off as a red light suddenly showed on the instrument panel in front of the pilot. "What's that mean?" Josh asked anxiously.

"It's a chip light," Keegan replied crisply, looking quickly below. "It means there's a problem with the tail rotor. Hang on, everybody! We've got to make an emergency landing—fast!"

Chapter Two

PREPARATIONS FOR DISASTER

At 5:30 that morning in Lihue,* a city nearly halfway around the island of Kauai from where Josh and Tank's helicopter was forced down, Tiffany Ladd awoke to the mournful wail of civil-defense emergency sirens. The last time she'd heard them, there had been a tidal-wave alert.

She turned on the bedside lamp and leaped to the floor. She almost collided with an open closet door before she realized she was in one of the guest bedrooms at Dr. and Mrs. Daniel Nakamura's spacious frame home.

Tiffany was a tall, slender high-school sophomore with short brunette hair and blue eyes. The plain gold cross suspended from a light chain about her neck bounced as she dashed into the hallway.

At the same time, her attractive mother, Mary Ladd, emerged from the adjacent bedroom wearing a flowered bathrobe. She snapped on the hallway light.

"What. . . ?" Tiffany started to ask, but was interrupted by Paula Nakamura opening her bedroom door and rushing into the hall. Her short, dark hair was in disarray. Tiffany's 10-year-old brother, Nathan, plunged into the hall, his eyes wide with fright.

"What is it, Mom?" he asked anxiously. Without waiting for an answer, the boy exclaimed, "I bet it's the hurricane!"

"Can't be!" Tiffany protested. "Yesterday at the Honolulu* Airport while we were waiting to fly here, I read a newspaper. It said Hurricane Iniki* was 385 miles southwest of the Big Island, and it was going to miss Hawaii."

Mrs. Nakamura replied, "I'll turn on the radio and find out." A short, stocky woman, she quickly tied a colorful silk robe about her waist. She hurried in bare feet along the strip of hallway carpet.

Followed by her guests, as the sirens continued their doleful sound, Mrs. Nakamura turned on the living room lamp and crossed the reed rug. She reached onto a shelf and punched a button on a radio.

Tiffany stood uneasily with her mother and brother as a male voice said from the speaker ". . . changed directions and is heading straight for Kauai, where it's expected to hit full force early this afternoon."

Mrs. Ladd said to Mrs. Nakamura, "John and your husband could be caught in the open!"

"What about Josh and Tank?" Nathan asked. "They're waiting for Dad and Dr. Nakamura on the beach."

"I'm worried about them too, but the authorities will probably evacuate that area, so the boys should be safe," Mrs. Ladd replied. "I'm not so sure about your father and Dr. Nakamura. They could be delayed and get caught in the open."

The announcer continued. "Iniki is now rated as a Category Four, with Five being the most dangerous kind. Hurricane Iwa* which hit Kauai 10 years ago was a Category One. Iniki's winds are expected to reach 200 miles an hour, making this the most powerful hurricane to hit the islands this century. Immediate preparations . . ."

Mrs. Nakamura turned the sound down. "Quickly, everyone get dressed! We must get ready!" She headed back toward the hallway.

"Paula!" Mrs. Ladd cried. "There's no way our husbands can know what's happening! If they get caught out in the open. . . !"

Mrs. Nakamura stopped and announced matter-of-factly, "Mary, we cannot help them, but we can help ourselves. Daniel and I lived through Iwa, so I remember what to do. Tiffany, please fill the bathtub in your room. I'll do the same in the master bedroom. We'll need that for drinking water. When you're all dressed, we'll do the other necessary things."

"Can't we do something about Dad?" Tiffany exclaimed after Mrs. Nakamura closed her bedroom door.

Mrs. Ladd said, "I'll phone the authorities to see if a helicopter can be sent to find them." She headed for the kitchen phone. "Tiffany, please fill the tub in your bedroom, as Paula asked."

Tiffany tried to swallow a lump that formed in her throat as she recalled the quarrel she'd had with Josh yesterday. *It was his fault*, she told herself firmly. *He shouldn't have been so stubborn!*

She was still angry with him as she reentered her guest bedroom, hurriedly scrubbed the bathtub and began filling it with water. Tiffany plopped down on the edge of the bed and slipped into a white tank top and shorts. She stepped into the straw sandals Mrs. Nakamura had provided for guests. In the Oriental fashion, nobody wore street shoes inside the house.

Tiffany sighed as the mournful sirens finally retreated into silence. A terrible possibility nagged at her. *What if they all die?*

She dismissed the thought, turned off the tub water and headed for the kitchen. Everyone else was already assembled there.

Tiffany looked expectantly at her mother. "Did you get through, Mom?"

"No, the helicopter people's lines are busy."

"Keep trying, Mom!"

"I will, Tiffany. Now, Paula, tell us what else needs to be done."

Mrs. Nakamura opened a cupboard door and removed a neatly typed list. "Daniel and I made this after the last hurricane," she explained. "We could go to a shelter, but I'm reluctant to leave our home. It survived one hurricane, so hopefully it'll do it again."

"We'll stay here with you," Mrs. Ladd decided.

Tiffany wanted to protest, *But this hurricane is a Category Four, not a One like Iwa was!*

Instead, she kept still, aware that she might never again see her father, her brother, Tank, or Dr. Nakamura.

Walking into the living room, followed by the others, Mrs.

Nakamura said, "Without Daniel, it's going to be hard to board up the windows and tie down or move everything that's loose outside of the house."

Nathan volunteered, "I can move the lanai* furniture into the garage."

"Fine, Nathan, if that's okay with your mother," Mrs. Nakamura replied.

When Mrs. Ladd nodded, Nathan raced out the front door, slamming it so hard the picture window vibrated.

Mrs. Nakamura scowled at the window. "There's no way we can board that up. Daniel had plywood over it last time, but without him, we'll just have to tape it."

"I can do that," Tiffany volunteered. "And all the other windows, too, if you have enough tape."

"My husband probably has plenty in the garage. Just make big Xs with the tape across the glass. But before you do that, Tiffany, let's go over what else has to be done." Mrs. Nakamura again consulted her list. "I should gas up the car, because nobody knows how long it'll be before any more is available after the storm.

"We're sure to lose electrical power, maybe for days or weeks. So we'll need to go to the grocery store for food that won't spoil quickly without refrigeration."

"If I may use your car, I'll get that," Mrs. Ladd said, "and try to buy gas."

"Good!" Mrs. Nakamura nodded approval. "We'll also need other supplies like bottled water, candles, flashlights and batteries. Ice, too—all you can get."

Tiffany's gaze drifted through the large picture window in the living room to the outside world. It was typically beautiful and clear, without any indication of the fierce winds and blinding rains that were forecast.

"Well, Mary," Mrs. Nakamura summarized, "if you'll head for the grocery store, Tiffany and I can begin on our safe place. When you get back, and Nathan has finished outside, we'll all tackle the mattresses."

"Mattresses?" Tiffany repeated.

"Yes. We'll pile them up around us as a barricade, sort of like a box with one end open. The mattress in our master bedroom is so heavy it'll take all of us to handle it. We'll also drag all the smaller mattresses off the guest beds into the master bedroom because it's the largest.

"We'll use mattresses to make a shelter high enough so we can all sit under them during the hurricane. There we'll be protected from flying glass in case the door or windows blow out."

Tiffany swallowed hard. "But your bedroom has a large sliding door opening to the lanai," she said. "Won't the wind come in if that door breaks?"

"It would, although we'll also tape and brace it. However, if that door does go, the wind could even tear off part of our roof. So we'll also prepare a backup safe place in the hall closet. It'll be cramped, but there are no windows."

Mrs. Ladd said, "I'll try the phones one more time first."

Tiffany watched her mother, thinking of the steps being taken in this house against the hurricane. She wondered what her father and Dr. Nakamura could possibly do to protect themselves if they were delayed in leaving the swamp.

Mrs. Ladd hung up the phone. "Still busy."

Mrs. Nakamura said, "I'll keep trying while you're at the store, Mary. Let's all get started."

After her mother drove away in the Nakamura's sedan, Tiffany entered the attached garage through the kitchen. She easily found masking and duct tape on wall pegboards. She took them, a pair of scissors, and an aluminum ladder to the outside of the big picture window that faced the street.

Nathan appeared from the back lanai area. His face showed fear as he ducked under some flowering plumerias* and stopped beside her. "Do you think they'll find Dad?"

"How should I know?" she snapped, setting up the ladder.

"You going to get mad at me like you did at Josh a couple of days ago?"

"It was his fault!" Tiffany blazed, pressing black masking tape as high as she could reach up the window. "Now, go finish what you're doing and leave me alone!"

As he walked away with head lowered, Tiffany was instantly annoyed with herself. She wasn't behaving the way she had been taught, but she excused herself because her emotions were running high.

She finished with the window and backed down the ladder just as the phone rang. "I'll get it," she called.

She raced inside and snatched up the living room phone. "Hello?" she said, hoping it was her father or brother calling.

Instead, a strange man's voice asked, "May I please speak to Mrs. Ladd or Mrs. Nakamura?"

Tiffany's hopes sank. "I'm Mrs. Ladd's daughter, Tiffany. Who's this?"

"I'm calling for Rainbow Helicopters."

"Are you calling about my dad or brother?"

The man hesitated before answering.

"Tell me! Has something happened to them?"

"One of our pilots radioed that he had picked up boys named Josh Ladd and Tank Catlett."

"That's my brother and his friend! What about them?"

"The pilot reported he was heading toward the Alakai Swamp to look for a Mr. Ladd and a Dr. Nakamura when they again landed and took aboard two strangers. . . ."

"What about my dad and brother?" Tiffany broke in.

The man hesitated, then said softly, "The helicopter disappeared from our radar screen."

"Disappeared?" Tiffany felt the blood drain from her face, and she felt faint. She asked in a hoarse whisper, "Does that mean they—crashed?"

She held her breath while waiting for the answer.

Chapter Three

SOME TERRIBLE DOUBTS

As the man on the phone still hesitated, Tiffany repeated in a frightened tone, "Does that mean their helicopter crashed?"

The man's voice in her ear sounded cautious. "Not necessarily." He paused again.

Tiffany covered the mouthpiece and yelled, "Mom!"

Nathan called, "She's not back yet."

"Mrs. Nakamura!" Tiffany screeched. She then lowered her voice somewhat and spoke again into the phone. "What do you mean — not necessarily?"

"Well, it could mean that the pilot suddenly decided to land. Or," the voice on the phone hesitated, then added softly, "it could mean he had some kind of emergency and was forced down in or near the swamp."

"Oh no!" Tiffany dropped the phone and turned away, burying her face in her hands. She knew about the hazards of Alakai Swamp from her father and Dr. Nakamura.

Mrs. Nakamura and Nathan arrived on the run as Tiffany

collapsed on the sofa. The woman took a quick look at the girl, then grabbed the phone and spoke into it.

Nathan plopped down beside his sister. "What happened?"

In a low, shocked tone, Tiffany repeated what she'd just learned.

"They crashed?" Nathan asked in disbelief.

"They don't know."

Mrs. Nakamura asked into the phone, "Can we rent another helicopter and look for them?" After a pause, she said, "Yes, I understand. But will you please keep us posted? Thank you."

She replaced the phone and sat down beside Tiffany and Nathan. She took them into her arms and spoke with assurance. "Just because they can't be reached by radio doesn't necessarily mean anything. Don't give up hope."

"What about Daddy?" Nathan asked in a weak tone.

"The man on the phone said the helicopter was flying toward the swamp, looking for him and my husband, when they lost contact with it. Both of them should have been out of the swamp by now and on the trail back."

"But what if they got a late start?" Nathan asked. "Could they get caught in the hurricane?"

Mrs. Nakamura replied, "I suppose they could. Naturally, I'm sick with worry for all of them, but there's nothing we can do. However, we can do something for ourselves. The hurricane will be here in a few hours, so we have to be ready."

The words seemed heartless to Tiffany, yet she also understood the truth in them. She wanted to curl up in a tight little ball of grief, but forced herself to rise and stumble outside.

The urgency of the double danger facing her family caused her to mount the ladder in a daze. She began taping windows, wondering how the Nakamura's beautiful home and yard would survive the hurricane.

The lawn was separated from the quiet residential street by a bougainvillea* hedge. Two coconut palm trees flanked the driveway. There were also hibiscus* and plumeria in bloom. A large mango* tree's dense foliage provided shade for the Nakamura's home.

Mr. Park, the next-door neighbor on the left, helped by two men, was hurriedly placing plywood across the windows. Tiffany studied the Parks' roof. *It looks old and in need of repair,* she decided.

Directly across the street stood Mrs. Yee's old dilapidated frame house. It seemed out of place in the upper-middle-class neighborhood. *I don't see how that one will survive in any kind of wind,* Tiffany thought.

Nathan approached and looked up at her. "I wish Mom would get back," he said.

"So do I," Tiffany admitted with a catch in her voice. "But there must be long lines everywhere."

"Do you think Josh is really dead?"

"No, of course not!" Tiffany spoke with a conviction she did not feel. "He's all right. So's Tank."

"What about Daddy and Dr. Nakamura?"

"Oh, hush up!" Tiffany cried. "How do I know?"

Nathan's lower lip quivered. "You don't have to bite my head off like you did Josh's yesterday!"

The words punctured Tiffany's momentary annoyance with her little brother. She climbed down the ladder to put her arms around him. "I'm sorry. I'm so tense."

He asked, "Don't you wish you'd done this to Josh after you yelled at him the way you did?"

The words sliced Tiffany's heart like a keen blade. She released Nathan. "It was Josh's fault," she said again, but with less conviction.

"What were you two arguing about?"

"Never mind. Just grab that stuff and help me with the next window."

Tiffany carried the light ladder around to the side of the house while Nathan followed with the tape and scissors. The tall glass window was closed, but the small narrow louvers on either side were open for ventilation. The radio newscaster's voice was clearly audible.

"While we're waiting for the latest information from authorities," he said, "here's a brief recap of the hurricane to this moment."

Tiffany didn't care. She was submerged in her emotional pain, and a nagging thought had begun to prick her conscience.

What if Josh was right, and I was wrong? Instantly, she shook her short dark hair in dismissal. That wasn't something she wanted to admit, not even now.

Subconsciously, she heard the newscaster's history of the storm bearing down on Kauai. "It started when two tropical disturbances formed off the west coast of Africa at about the same time. The first one developed into Hurricane Andrew that devastated Florida.

"The second one crossed the Atlantic, the Caribbean, Panama, and entered the Pacific. On September 8th, this became Hurricane Iniki. Our Hawaiian dictionary defines the word as meaning sharp or piercing, as wind or pangs of love."

Nathan commented, "It was supposed to miss Hawaii." He squinted at the sky. "On the news last night, they said the hurricane was passing the Big Island and going to pass Kauai today."

"I know. This is the second time Iniki fooled the forecasters. Yesterday I read in the Honolulu newspapers that it probably wouldn't affect the islands except for causing a high surf. Then it changed directions, and now we're going to have the worst hurricane of this century."

Tiffany folded the ladder and picked it up. "Come on, you can help me do the other side."

The newscaster's voice followed them through other louvered windows. "A hurricane has wind speeds of at least 74 miles an hour. Iniki's are forecast to be between 200 and 225 miles an hour when it slams into Kauai today."

Tiffany shook her head as she set the ladder under the next window. "Yesterday the news said we could expect thunderstorms north of this island but the hurricane was not likely to hit us. Now look what's happened."

As Tiffany applied rolls of tape to the glass, she periodically studied the sky, unable to believe what was coming. The familiar trade winds had withdrawn as though aware that they would be as nothing against Iniki's 225-mile-an-hour winds. The humidity was oppressive.

Tiffany finished the last window and vainly glanced down the street in hopes of seeing her mother returning. When she didn't, she and Nathan hurried inside the house to ask Mrs. Nakamura what they could do next.

"Let's see," Mrs. Nakamura said, "the bathtubs are filled, and I'm washing all the clothes. I guess we'd better get the smaller mattresses off the guest beds and into the master bedroom. Then let's find a safe place for my good china. I'm afraid it'll be blown off the shelves."

Tiffany and Nathan started to follow her down the hall when they heard a car drive up.

"Mom!" Nathan yelled, and started running to meet her.

"Nathan, wait!" Tiffany's sharp command stopped him. "Don't blurt out the news about the helicopter!"

Mrs. Nakamura hurried past the children. "Perhaps I should tell your mother," she said quietly. They followed her out the side door toward the car.

"What a madhouse!" Mrs. Ladd exclaimed, her arms full of supplies. "Lines to the service station stretch for blocks, and the stores are closing early so they can try to protect the windows and get home to their families. I could only . . . " she broke off suddenly, staring in alarm at the others. "What's the matter?"

"Mary," Mrs. Nakamura began in a quiet voice, taking the bag of ice and groceries from her. "It's about Josh."

Tiffany had never seen such a stricken look on her mother's face as, she learned about the missing helicopter. She drew

Tiffany and Nathan to her and held them tightly until Mrs. Nakamura had finished.

Then Mrs. Ladd looked at Tiffany and Nathan from eyes suddenly bright with tears. "There's nothing in the world I want more right now than to keep holding you so we can comfort each other. But we've done all we can for Dad and the others. Let's finish doing whatever is possible to save our lives and this home."

In the bedroom, pictures were removed from the walls. Then two regular-sized mattresses were dragged in from other bedrooms. One was leaned against the bare wall, the other was placed against the side of the Nakamuras' king-sized bed.

With great difficulty, the huge mattress was wrestled off the bed and across the two smaller mattresses, forming a roof. Nathan said it looked like a big doghouse.

"Now," Mrs. Nakamura said as Tiffany and Nathan stood panting beside the mattresses, "will you children please bring the portable radio from the closet and put it under the mattresses? Get flashlights and batteries, too. Mary, let's you and I prepare the closet for a backup safe place."

As the two women went down the hallway, Nathan asked his sister, "Do you really think we'll need a second safe place?"

"Mrs. Nakamura is more experienced than we are."

The little boy's eyes widened in fear.

Tiffany hurriedly distracted him. She said, "Help me shove this chest in front of that sliding glass door."

After he complied, Tiffany walked out of the bedroom into the hallway.

Nathan followed. "If the helicopter landed safely, I wonder what Josh and the others are doing right now?"

"Who knows? I just hope they can all fly out of there before the storm hits," Tiffany replied.

"What if they don't?"

"They'll find shelter some way, so don't worry."

"In a swamp?" Nathan asked.

"There must be some place they could be safe."

"Will you still be mad at Josh if he doesn't ever come home again?"

Tiffany whirled angrily to face her little brother. "Don't talk like that! He'll come home, and so will Dad and Tank and Dr. Nakamura."

Nathan drew back slightly but held his ground. "You sure are touchy! What did Josh say that made you so mad?"

Tiffany started to reply, "None of your business," but checked herself.

Thinking of the argument made her sick inside. *Oh, why did it have to end like this?*

Chapter Four

SEARCH IN THE SWAMP

In the air over Alakai Swamp, Josh instinctively held his breath, bracing for an emergency landing. He glanced down fearfully, seeing a small jungle-like area. The helicopter rapidly descended, still under power.

When they had cleared the trees and passed over stunted brush toward an open area, Josh sighed with relief. Just a few feet above the ground, the failing tail rotor caused the aircraft to begin spinning to the left.

It hit hard on the skids, bounced, rocked, and seemed about to tip over. Then it slowly righted itself. Josh's head snapped forward over the instrument panel with its warning chip light. The seat belt kept him from hitting the panel or the plexiglass in front of him.

Keegan had already cut the power, so the engine and the

overhead rotor blade were winding down when Josh straightened up.

Josh glanced at Tank and exclaimed, "We made it!"

"Sure did!" the pilot replied. "Everybody okay?" When all four passengers said they were safe, Keegan unsnapped his seat belt and threw open the right front door. "Good! Lucky we could set down on this bog. Nothing else around here would support our weight. Okay, everybody out. I'll radio home base, then I'll see how long it'll take to get this ship up again."

Josh and Tank grabbed their tennis shoes and slid out of the aircraft's door onto soft, spongy ground.

Franks and Garcia followed with their backpacks and rain gear while the big man cursed the delay.

Josh reminded Franks, "At least we're alive."

Tank, who tended to pessimism, glanced at the sky, then added thoughtfully, "Yeah — for now."

In the excitement of the forced landing, Josh had momentarily forgotten the hurricane. Standing on the bog with Tank, Franks, and Garcia, Josh squinted skyward.

There was still no sign of the coming storm. However, the air was intensely hot and humid. The strange stillness Josh had noticed on the beach was also with them in this remote area.

Franks commented, "I recognize this place. It's just inside the Alakai Swamp at about the 4000-foot elevation. This time of year, the temperature should be in the fifties, not stifling hot like this. It's usually raining or misty and foggy. That's why Garcia and I carry rain gear." He motioned toward his garment with a piece of burlap sack showing in the pocket.

After Josh and Tank had brushed their bare feet off as best they could and pulled on their tennis shoes, Josh looked around with some anxiety. He had never seen such strange terrain.

The helicopter rested in an flat, open area about 75 feet wide. But about a quarter of a mile ahead Josh saw a dense jungle of stunted trees. Beyond the jungle, endless rough, razorback ridges rose into the muggy air.

Over countless centuries of geological time, erosion had left narrow mountaintops with drop-offs of 100 feet or more. It was a remote, lonely area. Josh felt a shiver ripple down his spine.

Franks leaned in the open helicopter door and demanded, "How you doing in there, Keegan?"

The pilot removed his headset. "The radio's knocked out from our hard landing."

"No radio?" Franks roared angrily. "You probably didn't send a distress call with our position before we went down, did you?"

Keegan explained in a quiet tone. "There wasn't time. When that warning light came on, I did what had to be done first: find a safe place to set down fast. This bog was the only possibility."

Franks shouted, "You mean nobody knows where we are, and we can't tell them?"

"That's right. It's not uncommon for that to happen in a rough landing. So the office will know where we were heading and that we're down. They won't know our condition or location. Do either of you men know about radios?"

Garcia said, "I'm a botanist,* not an electrician."

Franks growled, "I'm no electrician, either. Well, Keegan, if you can't fix the radio, can you repair the chopper so we can fly out before the hurricane hits?"

Josh saw the pilot's face darken, but he spoke calmly. "I'll see what I can do."

Josh looked at Tank, then both turned to the pilot. Josh asked, "What can we do to help?"

"Nothing, but thank you anyway, boys." He paused, then added, "Well, yes, there is something. We landed right beside the trail to the swamp. All four of you might scout around and see if there are signs of anybody having passed this way.

"Josh, your father and his friend might be close by. But don't go far or lose sight of this chopper. You can get lost mighty easy in this swamp. A couple of men did that a few years ago and were never seen again."

Franks complained, "I don't want to look for anybody. I just want to get out of here — fast."

Keegan assured him, "You're no more anxious than the rest of us. Now, I'd appreciate it if you all would leave me alone so I can concentrate on this rotor."

The two boys walked with Franks and Garcia toward the barely visible trail they'd been following from the air. The ground changed from spongy to slippery and muddy.

Josh worried about his father and Dr. Nakamura, then forced his thoughts back to something he'd heard Franks say to the pilot. "Because you're a botanist, Mr. Garcia, you must have been in this swamp before."

"Many times," the little man assured him.

"Do you work for a state or federal agency?"

Before Garcia could answer, Franks laughed.

Garcia seemed intimidated by his partner's attitude. The shorter man pulled his long, skinny neck down into his shoulders like a turtle withdrawing from danger within his shell.

Josh and Tank exchanged looks, not understanding.

"Here's the trail," Franks said, stopping to examine the ground. "Hard to see, and it's so narrow we'll have to go single file."

He glanced around, then exclaimed, "Maybe we're in luck. I see two sets of boot tracks. One set's big; one's small." He looked at Josh. "Your father a big man?"

"He's six feet tall. Dr. Nakamura's short, maybe only five-six or so."

"I know," Franks replied, again studying the tracks. "But I didn't realize he had such a small foot."

Josh absently wondered how Franks knew Dr. Nakamura, but the boy's attention focused on the tracks in the trail. It was extremely wet and muddy and obviously didn't get much use, yet two people had recently passed.

Josh examined the tracks, then pointed. "There's a dog track, but they don't have a dog."

"Probably a feral* one," Franks replied in his quick, self-assured way. "A domestic dog gone wild could have passed before or after these boot tracks were made."

"Are there wild dogs in this swamp?" Tank asked, glancing around at the inhospitable landscape.

"Lost hunting dogs live here," Franks assured him. "Wild

pigs in here can be hunted year around, so hunters hike in during the early morning with a pack of six or eight dogs. They're mostly hybrids, called poi* dogs. Sometimes one gets lost and goes wild to survive."

"Are they dangerous?" Tank asked anxiously, studying the dog's prints. They led into the jungle-like area.

"They can become aggressive." Franks stood up. "Come on, let's follow these prints. Stay on the trail, because if you step off, you can sink in muck up to your hips."

"Are there other wild animals in here?" Josh asked.

Franks led the way toward the start of the dense undergrowth. "Yes, besides the wild pigs and feral dogs, there are a few goats and lots of black rats."

As the ground underfoot became muddier and footing more uncertain, Josh looked ahead, hoping for signs of his father and his companion. But there was nothing except increasingly wild, primitive country.

Garcia explained, "Most of the trees in here are ohia lehua,* and o'lapalapa.* The ohia are the tallest at maybe 35 feet. Actually, swamp trees are literally drowning. Most trees are knee high or less. So . . ."

Franks interrupted, "Who cares? Shut up, Garcia."

Josh came to the little man's defense. "I'd like to know."

"Me too," Tank said.

Garcia gave his big partner a triumphant look and continued. "As you can see, this is all tropical, very lush with lots of mosses and tree ferns. These plants are almost all native. Many of the insects, plants, and birds are not found anywhere else in the world."

"Are you a botanist, too, Mr. Franks?" Tank asked.

"No, and Garcia really isn't either." Franks' comment caused his companion to shoot him an angry look. "Let's just say he's my assistant."

Garcia muttered, "You couldn't do a thing out here if it wasn't for me! I'm the one who put you on to. . . ."

"Shut up!" Franks' harsh words caused the shorter man to break off his sentence.

He cringed, but Josh saw the anger in Garcia's eyes.

Josh didn't like the tension between the two men. *What's going on here?*

Josh remembered the map he'd found on the floor of the helicopter. *How did it get there?* Then it hit Josh. *One of those men dropped it. Probably when those things fell out of Mr. Franks' raincoat pocket as he was getting into the helicopter. He overlooked it.*

Josh shook his head at the flood of thoughts. *But how did he get that map? Dad or Dr. Nakamura wouldn't have given it to either of those men, so they must have stolen it. But how? When?*

These thoughts instantly triggered others. *What if they did something terrible to Dad and Dr. Nakamura, and that's why they weren't on the trail as I expected?*

Josh had to get Tank's attention without the two men noticing. He started to turn toward Tank, who was last in line. Then Josh glanced back the way they had come and blinked in surprise. "Hey! I can't see the helicopter!"

The others turned around and looked.

"Don't worry," Franks replied. "I'm familiar with this area. We'll go through this little patch of jungle to where the trees are stunted. If we don't find those men by then, we'll turn back."

Josh was apprehensive about getting lost, but his concern for his father urged him to follow as the two men resumed walking. Again remembering the map he had found in the helicopter, Josh dropped back to where Tank brought up the rear of the column.

Making sure that the two men weren't looking, Josh lowered his voice. "Look what I found." He handed the map to Tank.

Tank studied the map, now soft from the humidity. Three small ink markings had bled through the paper.

"That's a photocopy of the government recreation map like the one Dr. Nakamura and your dad took with them on their trip. See the ridges, trails, and streams?"

"It's the very same map. Look." Josh's finger jabbed at the center. "There's the Alakai Swamp. Just inside the boundary here, somebody's written with ink the word, 'bog.' And to the right of that, 'first sighting.' Up toward the top, there's something so smudged I can only make out the last two letters: v-e."

"The pilot said we'd landed on a bog," Tank replied thoughtfully. "And 'first sighting' could mean where Dr. Nakamura found those rare birds. But what ends in v-e?"

"Could be lots of words."

Tank squinted at the inked notations. "Is that your father's handwriting?"

"No. Must be Dr. Nakamura's."

"Where did you get this?"

"Found it on the helicopter floor when we went into that steep dive over the last big mountain. I think it fell out of Mr. Franks' raincoat when he dropped it getting into the helicopter. But where did they get it?"

"Maybe they found your dad and Dr. Nakamura and robbed them of it," Tank said in an ominous tone.

Josh had thought of something even worse, but didn't want to admit that. He tried to sound positive. "I think it's more likely they sneaked into Dad's camp and stole it. Or it could have been dropped without Dad or Dr. Nakamura knowing it, and these men found it."

"Camping's not allowed in this swamp, but your dad and Dr. Nakamura had special permits. On the other hand, these men had camping gear. Maybe they camped in the swamp without permission."

"When we first saw them, they were outside the swamp, where camping is okay," Josh said. "They were headed out, so maybe they followed Dad and Dr. Nakamura into the swamp yesterday, sneaked into their camp last night and stole the map. Or maybe they did it early this morning while Dad and Dr. Nakamura were away from camp. If I'm right, and we're correct about these ink markings, then Dad and Dr. Nakamura must be close by."

"But why did those two want this map?" Tank asked.

"They must be poachers."

Tank's eyes lit up. "Yeah! If a certain bird from another

country was worth up to $100,000 on the black market, can you imagine how much a Hawaiian bird that's supposed to be extinct is worth?"

"Makes sense, doesn't it? They got the map, but obviously didn't find the birds. They must have decided to come back with the map to steal them later. Then, in the helicopter, they changed their minds and wanted to help search for Dad and Dr. Nakamura after his name was mentioned."

"Yeah! And remember a while ago Mr. Franks said he knew that Dr. Nakamura was a short man? Josh, this is getting scarier and scarier!"

The blond boy squinted nervously at the forbidding swamp and the two men walking ahead, and then looked skyward, from where the coming hurricane would soon strike. "We're in deep trouble. What're we going to do?"

"We'll think of . . ." Tank interrupted himself. "I heard a dog bark!"

Franks turned around and yelled, "Hey, kids! I think we've found them!"

Josh hurriedly shoved the map into his pocket. "I sure hope so, but I don't know where Dad got a dog."

"What if it's one of those wild ones, and it's vicious?" Tank asked anxiously.

Josh broke into a run. "We'll soon find out."

Chapter Five

HORRIBLE NEWS

Josh tried to maintain his balance as he ran on the muddy trail toward where they'd heard the dog bark. He said to Tank, running beside him, "I sure hope Dad and Dr. Nakamura are just ahead, although I don't know where they got that dog."

"I just hope he's not one of those wild ones that could attack us."

"He'd probably run, like any wild animal."

Tank brightened. "Yeah! That's right. If it's your dad and Dr. Nakamura, we can all get back to the helicopter and into Lihue to be with your mother and the others before the hurricane hits. I mean, *if* the pilot can get the chopper fixed in time."

Josh glanced ahead at Franks and Garcia, who were nearing the end of the open swamp area close to where the jungle started.

The men ahead slowed to a walk as the boot prints and dog tracks moved away from the muddy trail and into the swamp vegetation. Franks took the lead, with Garcia, Josh and Tank in single file slowly falling behind as the trail began to disappear.

It could be followed only by plastic markers that someone had put up to help guide hikers.

Josh listened for the dog to bark again, but heard nothing. There were only a few birds flitting about, but they did not sing. Josh wondered if they sensed the coming hurricane.

Josh's mind jumped, wondering how his mother, sister, and brother were preparing for the hurricane in Lihue. *Tiffany's probably bossing everybody around, as usual, especially Nathan. Lately she's really been hard to get along with.*

The memory of his argument with her yesterday hit him with such sharpness that he wished he could tell Tank. But before Tiffany had brought up the subject that had led to the disagreement, she had made him promise not to tell anyone, not even Tank.

Josh was roused from his reflections by Tank's alarmed voice. "Can you see the helicopter?"

Josh glanced back and saw only the lonely desolation of the swamp. "No, but Mr. Franks and Mr. Garcia know this area. They'll help us find our way back."

"I hope so, but I remember that the pilot said two men got lost in here and were never found."

"We'll be all right," Josh said reassuringly. He turned around again. "Let's catch up with . . . hey, where'd they go?"

Quickly Josh swept his gaze ahead, but there was no sign of either Franks or Garcia.

"They're gone, and we're lost!" Tank cried. "We're all alone and lost in this swamp!"

"Calm down," Josh said firmly. "Mr. Franks and Mr. Garcia must have gone into those trees, so . . . oh!"

He broke off and jumped back a step as a medium-sized brown and black dog burst through the undergrowth. The dog stopped, silently eyeing the boys from six feet away.

"Wild dog!" Tank whispered.

"Don't move!" Josh whispered back.

He guessed that the short-haired male poi dog was a cross between a pit bull and an airedale. His body was lanky, but his chest was wide and deep.

"What if he attacks?" Tank asked hoarsely. "There's not a stick or rock we could use to defend ourselves."

"I don't think we'll have to," Josh answered quietly. "See his neck? He's wearing a collar, and it's fairly new." Josh raised his voice slightly and called, "Here, boy. Come here."

The dog did not move, but slowly wagged his tail.

"See?" Josh asked his friend. "He's okay."

"You're right." A girl's voice from behind the boys made them whirl around. "His name's Kahu,* which means 'Guardian' in Hawaiian." She snapped her fingers, and the dog came obediently to sit by her muddy hiking boots. "You always stare like that?" she asked, a hint of laughter in her tone.

Josh and Tank exchanged startled looks, then turned again to face the girl. She was about his age, Josh thought, and *hapa-haole**—probably part Hawaiian and Chinese along with some Caucasian.*

She lightly touched her smooth, light brown face with her left hand. "Have I got mud on me? Is that why you two keep staring?" She glanced down at her tan shirt and matching walking shorts. "Or something on my clothes?" she continued in a teasing tone.

She raised her head so that soft dark hair spilled about her shoulders and a red backpack. "Oh, I know what it is," she added, her deep brown eyes holding a hint of mischief. "You swamp boys never saw a real live girl before!"

Josh regained his composure. At the same time, he saw a way to stop the delight she was obviously having in teasing him and Tank. "There's a hurricane coming!" he blurted.

A shadow of concern flitted across her eyes, then the smile returned. "Oh, sure!" she exclaimed with a hint of sarcasm. She glanced at the sky. "Those few clouds drifting in are common as mud in this area, where it rains a few hundred inches a year. A hurricane? Come on!"

Josh was annoyed. "Look, I'm telling you the truth!"

The girl studied Josh's face, then Tank's. "How would you know that?" she asked. "I don't see either of you carrying a portable radio or anything where you could get such news."

Josh quickly explained about the helicopter, looking for his father and Dr. Nakamura, Franks and Garcia, and following the big and little human footprints with the dog's tracks.

"Those are my father's and mine," she said soberly when Josh had finished. "And Kahu's." She absently patted the dog's head. "We haven't seen anybody else." She added, "My dad stopped to photograph some flowers."

Moments later a brown-skinned man of middle age with curly black hair and broad shoulders hurried toward them. A

35-millimeter camera swung from a fabric strap across his neck. He carried a brown backpack. His old hiking boots were caked with mud. He stuck out his hand and smiled at the boys.

"Aloha!*" he said heartily, taking Josh's hand and shaking it vigorously. "I'm Eddie Miha.* I see you've already met my daughter, Malama.* What a surprise to see you boys out here. You alone?"

"No, we're with two men," Josh motioned in the direction Franks and Garcia had gone. "And we're looking for my . . ."

Malama interrupted, "Daddy, they say there's a hurricane coming."

Josh nodded and briefly repeated what he'd told the girl. When he had finished, the man studied the sky.

"I should have guessed," he said thoughtfully. "It's been so unbearably hot when it should be downright cool. And the humidity . . ." He broke off his thought and asked instead, "How far's your helicopter from here?"

Josh glanced around uncertainly. "Well, it's in a bog, in a kind of open place. . . ."

"Dad and I know where it is," Malama interrupted. "It's right over that ridge."

Her father exclaimed, "Look! Two men are coming. Josh, is that your father and his friend?"

Josh glanced up, then sighed in disappointment. "No, that's Mr. Franks and Mr. Garcia." They were alone, which told Josh that they had not found his father or Dr. Nakamura. Josh closed his eyes in anguish. There was now little chance of finding his dad in time.

"That'll make six of us," Malama said. "Will there be room in the helicopter?"

"Holds seven, including the pilot," Tank replied.

After the two parties met and introductions were made, all six people hurried toward the helicopter. Suddenly, Josh stopped and held up his hand. "Listen!"

The sound of a helicopter engine starting up made everyone whoop with joy and break into a run. But in a few seconds, the sound changed.

"He's shutting it down!" Franks cried.

"He's probably just saving fuel until we get there," Josh answered, trying hard to sound convincing. However, his heart seemed to skip a beat as he continued running toward the aircraft.

His hopes lifted when the pilot saw them, wiped his hands on a rag, and motioned for them to hurry.

"We're going to make it!" Tank cried, lengthening his stride to fall in behind Franks, who was leading.

"He'd better have that thing ready to fly," Franks muttered darkly. "Those clouds are moving in mighty fast, and the wind's starting to kick up."

Josh hadn't noticed, but one quick glance confirmed the big man's words. For the first time, there was some sign that Iniki was fast approaching.

"Well, Keegan," Franks called to the pilot, "we heard the engine. Are you ready to take off?"

The pilot ignored the question, but looked at the two new-comers. "Introduce me to these two, and I'll tell you."

"That'll wait!" Franks roared. "Now tell me, did you fix this thing so it'll get us out of here or not?"

Josh saw the pilot's face set in firm lines and his eyes narrowed. "We'll know in a few minutes." He stuck out his right hand to Eddie Miha and introduced himself.

Franks yelled, "Let's get out of here!"

Josh saw the pilot's jaw muscles twitch with annoyance, but he smiled at the newcomers. "Mr. Miha, I assume you and your daughter would like to ride with us?"

"Call me Eddie. And yes, we certainly would. How about our dog?"

Keegan nodded. "Yes, if this bird flies. But you'd all better stay here until I'm ready."

"What about my father?" Josh cried in anguish, shifting his weight uneasily on the spongy ground. "I don't want to go without him!"

The pilot laid a hand gently on the boy's shoulder. "We'll look for him from the air, but time's running out for everyone. I know it's hard, but if we don't find him quickly, we have no choice but to leave the swamp." He gave Josh's shoulder a quick pat, then climbed into the aircraft.

Josh was too sick at heart to answer as the sun disappeared behind a cloud. The clear, beautiful sky was now being rapidly replaced by threatening dark clouds. They rolled across the heavens, driven by the advance winds of the coming hurricane.

"Let's hope this helicopter flies," Tank said quietly, "and we find your dad and Dr. Nakamura."

Josh nodded, keenly feeling the tension as the pilot began

the start-up process. Josh leaned close to Tank and lowered his voice so the others wouldn't hear. "My chest feels like an elephant's sitting on it."

"Mine too." Tank shook the blond hair out of his eyes and squinted at the sky. "But it's not just from being scared that the engine won't start. It's the humidity. I've never felt it so bad."

Josh nodded, aware that this was the most muggy, unpleasant day he'd spent on the islands. *Must be the hurricane. I wonder how long before it hits?*

He cast one final, desperate look around the swamp in hopes of seeing his father and Dr. Nakamura. But there was nobody else in sight.

He turned eagerly toward the aircraft when he heard the engine begin to turn over. *Come on, come on! Start!*

It did, causing the six people on the ground to let out a collective yell of joy. That faded into disappointed groans as the motor died.

"What's the matter, Keegan?" Franks yelled, striding to the helicopter's open right door. "That motor sounded fine to me! Why'd you shut it down again?"

"The warning chip light came on again."

"Meaning what?" Franks demanded hotly.

"Meaning," Keegan replied bluntly, "there's no way we can fly out of here. So we'd better find shelter fast—or we're all going to die in the hurricane!"

Chapter Six

THE POACHERS

Franks yelled at the pilot, "What do you mean, there's no way we can fly out of here?"

"Just what I said," Keegan replied. "This chopper isn't airworthy, so we'd better find shelter fast."

Josh looked quickly at Tank, Malama, her father, Franks and Garcia, then back to the pilot. "You sure?"

"Positive. This bird's not going up without a part, and we're not going to get one out here."

Tank asked in a frightened, hoarse voice, "What're we going to do? There's no shelter in this place!"

Malama spoke up. "Maybe there is." She turned to her father. "Dad, isn't there a cave around here. . . ?"

"Cave?" Garcia interrupted, stretching his long neck hopefully. "Where?"

Eddie Miha pointed. "That way. Thirty minutes walk."

Josh eagerly followed the extended hand, but Franks loudly proclaimed, "I know something closer! There's an old cabin not far from here, in the same direction. Used to be a water gauge station run by the government to measure flow in the stream. Let's go. . . ."

"I've seen that place," Eddie interrupted. "It's on the way to the cave, but it's not safe."

Keegan added, "I've also seen that shack. It's about 30-years old. I don't think it'll stand up to a Category Four hurricane. If Eddie knows about a cave . . ."

Franks broke in, "That cabin is sure better than being out here in the open. Besides, it's too far to that cave over very rough country. I say we head for the shack before the storm catches us. Come on, everyone."

"Wait!" the pilot said crisply. "I think a person would be safer under an ohia log than in that shack during a hurricane. I favor heading for the cave."

The tension between the two strong-willed men was almost as oppressive to Josh as the intense humidity. Eddie commented sadly, "I hate to see us split up, because we may need each other before this thing is over, but Malama and I are going to the cave."

"You'll never make it!" Franks warned. "Come on, Garcia. You boys better come with us."

Tank looked at Josh. "What do you think?"

"I think we should go with the girl and her dad."

Franks' face flushed. "You're all fools," he snapped, and turned away. "Let's move, Garcia."

As the two men hurried away across the bog, Josh remembered the map they had dropped getting into the helicopter earlier. They apparently hadn't missed it yet.

The pilot's words broke into Josh's thoughts. "Eddie, lead us to that cave."

Eddie nodded and started off with his daughter. Keegan motioned for Josh and Tank to go next. He brought up the rear.

Josh glanced anxiously at the sky. The most dark, ominous clouds he'd ever seen were moving in fast. Gusts of wind began whipping the low-growing trees and shrubbery, but the intense humidity remained unchanged. After a few steps, Josh was again perspiring freely.

He kept his eyes moving, hoping to see some sign of his father and Dr. Nakamura, but there was no one else in sight except Franks and Garcia. They were about a hundred yards away. Suddenly, they left the trail and plunged into the under-brush, moving toward a ridge.

Josh asked, "Why are they doing that? If they're taking a shortcut, they could get lost."

"They won't get lost, Josh," Eddie replied.

"How do you know that?"

"Because," Eddie answered, "those two men know this country. You see, they're bird poachers."

Startled, Josh increased his pace until he was only a step behind the father and daughter. "They are?"

"Yes. I've seen them before." Eddie turned serious brown eyes on Josh and Tank, who had caught up with him again.

Josh frowned thoughtfully. "When you were introduced," he commented, "neither they nor you let on that you knew each other."

"Oh, we had never actually met, but Malama and I have seen them before here in the swamp."

"Didn't they also see you?" Josh wanted to know.

Eddie shook his head. "No, we kept out of sight."

Tank asked, "Have either of you seen those men capture any birds?"

"No," Eddie replied, "but I've seen their traps."

"Dad destroyed them," Malama added with satisfaction. "We'd like to turn those men in to the authorities, but it would be our word against theirs. So Dad hopes someday to get pictures of the men setting the traps. That would be proof."

They walked on while Josh wondered if Malama and her father had ever seen the rare birds Dr. Nakamura had found. Josh asked, "What kinds of birds are they after?"

Eddie answered, "Obviously not the common native forest birds within the swamp, but very rare ones."

"There are six of those rare birds here in the Alakai Swamp," Malama added. "They include the Kauai 'o'o'a'a. . . ."

Josh didn't hear any more. *That's the same bird that Dr. Nakamura took Dad to photograph,* he thought. But he had to be sure. He asked, "Isn't that the black one with the yellow thigh feathers that the ancient Hawaiians used to make their feathered capes and helmets?"

"That's right," the girl replied. "I'm surprised you know that."

"I've seen them in the Bishop Museum at Honolulu."

Eddie explained, "The 'o'o birds are critically rare. Confirmed sightings haven't been made since the last hurricane ten years ago. The birds may be extinct."

Maybe not, Josh thought, thinking of his father and Dr. Nakamura. *Oh, Lord! Please take care of them. And Mom and Nathan and Tiffany, too.*

* * *

Trailed by her little brother, Tiffany walked down the hallway of the Nakamura house toward the kitchen. She tried hard to stop the memories of her argument with Josh. But her last angry words to him echoed in her mind.

I don't ever want you to talk to me again, Josh! So shut up!

"Shut up!" Tiffany said aloud.

Nathan protested, "I didn't say anything!"

Aware that she had unintentionally spoken aloud, Tiffany bent quickly and whispered, "I didn't mean you!"

"There's nobody else around but me."

"I was thinking of what I'd said to Josh."

"Do you know what Mom and Dad would say if they heard you say 'shut up' to anybody?"

"I know," Tiffany glanced nervously toward the open kitchen door, "but it was none of Josh's business."

Nathan complained, "You sure have been acting cranky lately. What's wrong with you?"

"There's nothing wrong with me!" she snapped, eyes blazing. "I'm just growing up, that's all!"

"You're only fourteen."

"Well, that's practically grown, and I've got a mind of my own."

"You sound like you've been listening to that Rusty guy too much."

Tiffany shoved her face close to Nathan's. "What do you know about him?" she demanded in a whisper.

Drawing away, Nathan replied, "I first saw him when he moved into the apartment building next to ours. Then I saw you talking to him when he was polishing his surfboard. That's when he said that you're practically grown and should have a mind of your own."

"You were spying on me?"

"No, I just happened to overhear." Nathan paused, then added, "Mom has seen you talking to him too. I don't think she likes him, because I overheard her telling Dad the other night. They don't like him hanging around."

"They haven't said anything to me."

"Josh says that's because they don't want you to defend him. They hope you'll lose interest in him."

"What else did Josh tell you?"

"Nothing, only I don't think Josh likes Rusty any more than I do."

"What do you two know about him?"

"I know he doesn't believe like we do, and I don't like the looks of those guys he hangs out with, either."

"They're free spirits!"

"Look, I don't want to get into an argument the way you

and Josh did." Nathan paused, his eyes narrowing thoughtfully. "That's really what you two got into it about, isn't it? Rusty!"

"None of your business!"

* * *

In the swamp, Malama had warmed to her subject. "There's a lot of money in poaching rare birds and selling them on the black market. It's illegal, of course, but some private collectors in foreign countries will pay gobs of money for a special bird."

Her father added, "There are many birds in this swamp, but they haven't been singing much today. Maybe they sense the coming hurricane."

"Are you an ornithologist?" Tank asked.

"No, I'm just a man who loves birds, especially those in the swamp area."

The group fell silent for a few moments before Tank asked anxiously, "How much farther to the cave?"

"Another few minutes," Eddie answered. "You tired?"

Josh saw his friend steal a glance at the girl before vigorously shaking his head. "Who, me? No."

"Good," Eddie replied. "We're going to leave the bog in a few minutes. This is where the vegetation is sort of like Alaskan tundra. It's mushy, with sedges and mosses growing everywhere. Notice how your feet squish when you walk? Well, we're coming to a section where you can sink to your knees or hips."

"But," his daughter added hastily, "you can usually see the standing water and go around it."

Josh anxiously wondered if they would be able to reach the cave in time. As if to stress the urgency and doubt, the sun disappeared behind a cloud.

Josh saw that Franks and Garcia were still out of sight. So far as Josh could see, there was nobody or nothing else in view.

Kahu, the dog, trotted a few feet, then suddenly plunged off the trail.

Malama asked softly, "What's he after, Dad?"

"I don't know."

Tank whispered fearfully, "Wild pig, maybe, or goats. Or one of those hunting dogs gone wild."

The dog reappeared, carrying a red-billed cap in his mouth. Malama retrieved it. "Some hunter lost . . ."

Josh interrupted. "Let me see that, please."

He took the cap from the girl and turned it over.

"It's my dad's! See? His name's inside. That means he's somewhere nearby. I've got to look for him."

"Sorry, Josh," Eddie said firmly. "If you stop, the hurricane will catch you. Let's all keep going."

Josh hesitated, torn between the tremendous desire to find his father and the necessity of getting under shelter, fast.

Josh held his father's red-billed cap and glanced around hopefully. "He's *got* to be someplace close by," Josh told the others.

"Yeah," Tank agreed, "but where? This is a mighty big old swamp, and that hurricane's coming fast."

Josh nodded thoughtfully, looking at the pilot, Eddie Miha, and his daughter. Their eyes all showed their personal fear of being delayed and caught in the open.

"I know," Josh responded with a sigh of resignation. "I guess you're right. Let's go on to the cave."

Tank said hopefully, "If it's the only shelter around, maybe your dad will be there."

Josh's face brightened. "I hadn't thought of that! Come on, let's hurry!"

Chapter Seven

WHEN A BROTHER AND SISTER QUARREL

In the Nakamura's house Tiffany glared at her little brother and repeated, "It's none of your business! Do you hear me?"

He ignored her implied threat. "You can't fool me. You and Josh argued about Rusty, huh?"

Tiffany was annoyed with Nathan, but sometimes when he took hold of something, he wouldn't let go. She glanced toward her mother and Mrs. Nakamura, who stood facing the kitchen cupboards, their backs to Tiffany and Nathan.

Tiffany had to be careful. "I can't tell you," she said to Nathan in a low, annoyed whisper. "I made Josh promise he wouldn't tell, either."

"Did *you* promise not to tell anybody?"

"No, of course not."

"Then you can tell me."

Tiffany threw up her hands in disgust.

Mrs. Ladd saved the moment by calling, "What are you two whispering about? Come and help us."

Sighing with relief, Tiffany started to obey, but a final

glance at her little brother convinced Tiffany that he wasn't through pestering her about this.

The front doorbell rang. "I'll get it." Tiffany whirled about, anxious to be away from Nathan.

She opened the front door and blinked in surprise. "Rusty!" she exclaimed, looking over her shoulder in alarm. She stepped outside and pulled the door shut.

The tall, barefooted boy of about sixteen wore only faded cutoffs. He held a surfboard under his right arm. Long, stringy blond hair fell across his thin, heavily freckled shoulders.

Tiffany noticed the five-pointed, star-shaped symbol he always wore on a chain about his neck. She forgot what he had told her it was called. When she once asked what it meant, he merely shrugged. She had intended to look it up in the diction-ary but could only remember how the word started: *Penta.*

"Hi!" he greeted her with a grin. "Bet you didn't expect to see me, huh?"

"I thought you were in Honolulu," she replied, flustered at seeing him and anxious because she didn't want her mother or brother to know Rusty was here. At the same time, she man-aged a friendly smile.

"I was." He swept his free hand toward the street. "You remember my buddies?"

Tiffany waved at the three other teenage boys who sat in an old rusted sedan. They waved back.

At the same time, Tiffany was aware of other cars moving rapidly past with plywood strapped to the roofs, or trunks tied down over huge loads of groceries and emergency supplies.

The air was stifling, and the humidity was so high Tiffany realized she had a light sheen of perspiration on her upper lip. She discreetly brushed it away before Rusty could see.

As he turned to face her again, she blurted, "There's a hurricane coming. Don't you know about it?"

He shrugged. "Oh, sure, but it's no big deal." He cocked one eyebrow and asked in a low voice, "When are you going to sneak out on a date with me?"

"Shh!" Tiffany felt a twinge of guilt along with her excitement at seeing him. "You know how my parents feel about dating."

"You're old enough to know your own mind," he said, lightly running his left index finger along her jaw.

Tiffany changed the subject, fearful her mother or brother would see her talking to Rusty. She asked, "Are you going to tell me what you're doing here?"

He grinned at her from a thin face that was more freckled than tan. "Why," he said flippantly, "I came to see you, of course."

She wanted to believe that, but knew better. "No, really," she prompted.

He shrugged. "A couple days ago my old man gave me the money to fly over here to surf with these guys. . . ." He paused, studying her face. "Why'd you flinch?"

"I don't like hearing you call your father 'my old man.' It's not respectful."

Rusty laughed. "See? There you go again! You're so hung up that you're afraid to be your own person like I am. You have to get over that if you're going to grow up and join the real world."

"I have to go back inside," she insisted nervously. "So why did you come?"

He turned to glance at his three friends in the car and explained. "We're all living in sort of an old place outside of town, but the authorities say we can't stay there because it'll probably get blown to pieces when Iniki comes. You'd told me that you were going to be here with the Nakamuras, so . . ."

"You need a safe place to stay," she interrupted, in sudden panic. She could ask Mrs. Nakamura, but Tiffany's mother wouldn't like the idea, even though she might not say anything under the circumstances.

"Actually, no," Rusty replied. "We have a safe place lined up, but there's no room for my surfboard. So I want to shove it under this house until the hurricane is over."

It wasn't a request for permission, but a statement of what was wanted. *That's just like Rusty,* Tiffany thought. She considered asking Mrs. Nakamura, but didn't want her mother to know Rusty was anywhere around.

"Okay," Tiffany decided, looking around to make sure nobody was watching. "Go around behind of the house that way," she pointed in the direction where anyone inside would be unlikely to see him. "Shove it under the back lanai. Be very quiet. When you come to get it after the storm, try not to let anybody see. . . ."

"Tiffany! Tiffany!" Rusty said reprovingly. "You've got to

learn to quit caring what other people think." He hoisted the surfboard. "See you around."

She was still flustered upon reentering the kitchen where her mother looked up from loading the dishwasher. Nathan and Mrs. Nakamura were not in sight.

"Who was at the door?" Mrs. Ladd asked.

"Uh . . ." Tiffany stalled, annoyed because she should have anticipated the question. "Just some guy."

"What'd he want?"

Tiffany didn't meet her mother's eyes. Lying was against the girl's beliefs, but she decided to slant the truth slightly. "He asked directions."

Well, it's true, Tiffany assured herself to ease the pang of conscience that zapped her. "I'll vacuum the living room," she volunteered, wanting to avoid further questioning. The noise of the cleaner would prevent that, and she could be alone with her thoughts.

Shoving the vacuum cleaner back and forth, Tiffany recalled how she and her girl friends at home had often talked and giggled about boys. Tiffany had never really cared much about them until Rusty came along.

What made him appealing, she decided, was that he was different, more daring than the boys she knew at school or Sunday school. He wore his hair longer than Josh, Tank, Nathan, or any boy Tiffany knew. Rusty also looked at her in a way no other boy had. She liked that, but it made her want to shiver just a little, too.

Nathan entered the room and motioned for her to turn off

the vacuum. There was something about his expression that made her obey. She followed him to the front door.

He motioned for her to bend down. When she did, he said softly, "I saw Rusty putting his surfboard under the back lanai."

"So?" Her tone was low and defensive, yet she felt a certain fear. *If Nathan's going to tell. . . .*

"So I know who was at the front door."

"What of it?"

"I heard what you told Mom just now. She wouldn't like it if she knew you lied to her."

"I didn't lie!"

"Dad says that when a person wants to do something that's wrong, the first thing they do is lie to themselves. That's what you're doing."

"I am not!" Her voice rose in spite of herself. She glanced anxiously toward the kitchen. Her mother was not in sight. Mrs. Nakamura was in the laundry room where she couldn't hear.

"How'd you meet this guy, Rusty, anyway?"

"None of your business."

Nathan grinned and reached into his pocket. He pulled out something on a chain. "Look what I found," he said. "Rusty must have dropped it putting his board under the lanai. What is it?"

Tiffany recognized the five-pointed, star-shaped symbol Rusty had worn about his neck. "Give me that!" She tried to snatch it away.

Nathan jerked it out of reach. "No, no! I think I'll give this to Mom. Maybe she'll know what it is."

"You're awful!" Tiffany hissed, knowing that she couldn't draw her mother's attention to the scene.

Nathan grinned broadly. "I'm a good listener."

Fighting back her annoyance, Tiffany explained. "I can't remember what it's called. Penta-something."

"Okay, now we're getting somewhere. How did you meet Rusty?"

She lowered her voice and glanced uneasily toward the kitchen. "At the beach. Remember when Ashley Crawford was visiting from the Mainland?"

"Uh-huh." Nathan made a face, remembering with distaste the blonde 16-year-old.

All the older boys who lived in the apartment building where the Ladds and Catletts did had made fools of themselves over Ashley. But Nathan, at 10, wasn't impressed with girls.

Ashley had come with her parents in August, and, just as everybody did when they arrived in Hawaii, they called the people they knew who lived in the islands.

Even if they had only been casual acquaintances on the Mainland, visitors always acted as if you were long-lost best friends. That usually got them a tour of the islands' sites, a dinner or two, and sometimes a few nights as house guests.

The Ladds' apartment was too small for overnight guests, but Ashley and her parents had received all the other amenities. That included Tiffany taking Ashley to the world-famous Waikiki Beach* a couple miles from the Ladds' apartment.

Nathan prompted, "I remember her. So?"

"Ashley and I were getting a tan when some boys waded ashore and stuck their boards upright in the sand by us. Right away, they all started talking to Ashley— all except one. He talked to me. That was Rusty.

"I found out he'd just moved into the apartment building next to ours. His folks are divorced. He lives with his dad, who's a salesman and is gone a lot to the neighboring islands."

"How come you never invited him to Sunday school like some other kids who live in the apartments?"

Tiffany closed her eyes, remembering how she had done that and the way Rusty had kidded her.

His words echoed in her mind. *Sunday school is for kids. You're old enough to stop going. After all, you're sixteen.*

Tiffany winced, remembering the lie she'd told him that first day on the beach. It had just popped out, and later, it had backfired.

Rusty thought she was old enough to date, and she didn't want to tell him differently. He thought she was simply afraid of her parents and kept urging her to sneak out with him.

Seeking support that she knew would never come from her parents, she had approached Josh, expecting him to understand and support her. Instead, he had listened, then been quick and firm in his decision. "Forget it!"

That wasn't what she wanted to hear, so she had blown up. Her angry remarks had led to their quarrel.

Now the helicopter he had flown in with Tank was down somewhere in Kauai's remote interior. Was he alive or dead?

Tiffany felt she was somehow responsible. At least she knew she shouldn't have let him go off with angry words between them. And if her father was also lost . . .

She wanted to pray, but could not. She hadn't been able to do that since that day on the beach.

Josh! Tiffany thought with a groan. *If you're alive, how are you going to survive the hurricane?*

Chapter Eight

SECRET OF
THE OLD SHACK

E ddie Miha again took the lead toward the cave, followed single file by his daughter, the helicopter pilot, Tank, and Josh.

Now the last person in line, Josh kept looking in all directions, hoping to see some sign of his father. Josh guessed that Franks and Garcia had reached the shack.

Questions buzzed through Josh's mind as he glanced down at his father's red-billed cap. *How long ago did he drop this? Maybe this morning? Where is he? And Dr. Nakamura? Do they know a hurricane's coming, or will they be caught in the open when it hits?*

There were no answers as the small party struggled up the increasingly rugged terrain. There was now no trail, nothing but a tangle of logs and brush Eddie said had been there since the last hurricane.

The way became very steep, so at the top of another ridge, they stopped to catch their breath.

The clouds were so dark that it seemed more like the coming

of night than the middle of the day. The rising wind made a low, moaning sound and whipped the low-growing brush and trees. Their limbs rattled like dry bones clacking together.

Tank said quietly to Josh, "I sure hope Eddie knows where he's going."

Malama, from her place just ahead of the boys, turned and smiled reassuringly. "You haole* boys can rest easy. Dad knows the way."

"Yeah," Tank replied a little sharply, "but can he get us there before the storm starts?"

Josh turned to give his friend a warning look. He didn't want to create any hard feelings with the girl or her father.

Malama said cheerfully, "We'll make it."

Tank grumbled but lapsed into silence.

Malama spoke to her father, who turned and faced the boys. "We're almost there. Just around that bend up ahead we drop down to a little stream. After we cross that, it's just up the next hill. A few minutes."

They continued their trek, carefully picking their way and trying to keep from sliding on the muddy ground.

Josh caught sight of the little stream. "This water looks like tea," he observed.

Eddie explained, "That's due to the tannic acid leached from the ferns."

Josh was in the middle of wading across the tea-colored water when he glanced upstream, then stopped. "Hey, Tank, look over there. That must be the shack where Franks and Garcia were heading."

Keegan turned around from where he stood on the bank with Eddie and Malama. "You're right. See how flimsy it looks? I hope they don't regret having decided to go there instead of with us to the cave."

Tank commented, "At least it's shelter."

"Yes," Malama replied, "but for how long?"

The others started on toward the cave, but Josh still studied the windowless shack, barely visible in the thickening gloom.

"What if my father and Dr. Nakamura are in there?"

"They've got no way of knowing about that place." Tank assured him. "Let's move!"

"It's true that Dad wouldn't," Josh agreed, "but Dr. Nakamura might. And we know they were nearby because of finding Dad's cap. I'd like to take a quick look, just in case that's where they are."

Tank started to protest, "Aw, Josh. . . ."

He interrupted. "It will only take a minute. The rest of you go on. I'll follow your tracks."

Eddie tilted his face to the sky before answering. "I'm afraid to chance your getting lost, Josh."

"I'll be fine," he assured them. "I've just got to make sure that Dad's not in that shack."

Eddie glanced at Keegan, who nodded.

"Okay," Eddie said, "we'll wait here a few minutes."

"Be right back!" Josh whirled to the right and started running as fast as his muddy shoes allowed.

Tank called a warning. "Watch out for Franks and Garcia!"

"I'll be careful."

"Remember that other thing!" Tank called.

What other thing? Josh asked himself, hurrying on. *Oh, the map!*

He hadn't thought of the map that Franks and Garcia had dropped. *I wonder what they'd do if I ran into them and they knew I had it?*

Josh plunged through the ferns, jumped logs and smashed brush underfoot, his mind now mixed with hope for his father and fear of the two poachers.

Who's going to be in that old shack? What secrets does it hold? I've got to find out fast.

A few minutes later Josh neared the cabin which stood in a small clearing with ohia trees all around. One ohia, about two feet in diameter and taller than the others, grew directly over the shack.

The building was only about six by ten feet, Josh guessed. The roof and sides were made entirely of aluminum with a dia-mond-shaped pattern. It was not rusted, which surprised Josh because of the heavy rains that fell year-round.

The roof was covered with bits of limbs and twigs that had fallen from the overhead tree. The structure was battered and bent, apparently from strong winds over the years. It looked cold and uninviting, but it offered possible shelter.

As he drew near, hoping against hope that his father was within, Josh suddenly stopped with a fearful thought.

What if Dad and Dr. Nakamura are in there with Franks and Garcia? What if they took them prisoners to make them tell where the rare birds are? They wouldn't need the map if that happened.

The possibility sent little ripples of gooseflesh over Josh's shoulders and down his arms. He stood silently contemplating the shack. It was very quiet and somehow threatening.

Josh stepped cautiously over bits of broken limbs and stopped in front of the door made of two-by-fours.

"Anybody here?" he called, then listened, but heard no response. *Hmm. Franks and Garcia should be here by now, so why don't they answer?*

Josh again called out and waited. He heard nothing but the rising wind now moaning among the ohia trees. It was a lonely, scary sound.

Josh started to call out for the third time, then jerked nervously when something thumped against the shack's roof. He jumped back, almost tripping over brush underfoot. He was greatly relieved to see a small piece of dead wood roll off the roof and fall at his feet.

Josh pushed against the door. It squeaked like something from a scary old movie. The door opened a couple more inches on very rusty hinges.

Josh heard another squeak and looked down. A black rat slipped through the opening door. The rodent climbed the nearest tree with amazing speed.

If rats are in here, Josh decided, shoving the door open more forcefully, *then probably no human's in here. Including Dad and Dr. Nakamura. But I've got to be sure.*

The gloom inside the shack was even worse than that created

outside by the hurricane's approach. Josh first saw a potbellied, wood-burning stove. He decided that it must get cold inside, although now it was very hot.

In the gloom Josh also saw a pile of rope, three old cots against the far wall, and a bucket that probably was used to carry water from the stream. There were no chairs, no table, and no lights.

Disappointed in not finding any sign of his father, Josh stepped inside for a final look. He stared at a dark shapeless object in the corner. For a moment, he thought it might be a person slouched there.

Then something leaped out and streaked across the splintery wooden floor straight at Josh. Instinctively, he leaped aside, but not before two more black rats scurried across his foot and out the open door. Josh shook off a shiver. He knew they wouldn't hurt him, but he found them repulsive.

Walking carefully in case there were more rodents, Josh approached the object in the corner.

He whirled in alarm as the door squeaked shut, then laughed nervously at his reaction. He turned around and bent to examine the object in the corner more closely.

An old sleeping bag, Josh decided, straightening up. *It's probably a rat's nest now* .

Satisfied that his father wasn't there, Josh clomped noisily across the splintery wooden floor toward the door. As he reached for the handle, the door opened so fast Josh had to jump back to keep from getting hit.

The door's edge brushed against him, knocking the map

from his shirt pocket. It fell to the floor because all Josh's attention focused on Franks and Garcia, who pushed their way into the room.

"Hi!" Josh exclaimed, fighting off a ripple of fear. "I wondered why you weren't here already."

"We had slow going," Franks replied, squinting into the room's gloomy interior.

Garcia whispered, "We got lost."

"Shut up!" Franks snapped without looking at the shorter man. "Where are your friends, Josh?"

"Waiting for me downstream."

"Still heading for that cave?" Franks shook his head in disapproval. "You'll never make it. That hurricane's coming on fast."

"We'll be okay," Josh said, starting out the door.

"You dropped something," the short man said, bending quickly.

The map! Josh's heart leaped wildly. Quickly, the boy reached out to retrieve it, but Garcia held on.

"Where did you get this, Josh?" he demanded suspiciously, handing it to his partner.

"Uh . . ." Josh stammered, debating whether to try and explain or run away.

Franks took one quick glance at the map, then kicked the door shut. "You got some explaining to do!"

Josh fought to speak around the rock that suddenly seemed to appear in his throat. "I have to be going." As he reached for the door, Franks knocked his hand down. "You're not going anywhere, kid!"

At that instant, the first big gust of wind shook the shack and rain started drumming on the metal roof.

Hurricane Iniki left no doubt that it had arrived.

Chapter Nine

A BOLD-FACED LIE

Nathan's curiosity about Rusty was upsetting Tiffany, but she tried to keep calm even when he persisted in his questions.

"How come," Nathan asked again, "you never invited Rusty to Sunday school like the other kids who live in the apartments?"

"Lots of reasons," she replied evasively. She looked out the big front picture window of the Nakamura's home and tried to change the subject. "That old house across the street sure looks out of place in this subdivision."

Nathan joined her, peering through the tape that had been stretched across the window. "Mrs. Nakamura said that it belongs to Mrs. Yee."

"I heard. She's an old widow who bought the house years ago before this subdivision was built. She's been on the Mainland for a while."

Tiffany took a good look at the Yee house. Although it

stood in an upper-middle-income residential area, it was totally unlike the large four-bedroom home owned by the Nakamuras and other homes nearby.

The Yees' frame home was narrow, like a trailer home on the Mainland. At most, the gray building was 50 feet long. The windows had been boarded for a long absence. The rusted corrugated sheet roof had a slight pitch to let the rains drain off.

The detached, single-car garage was made entirely of rusted, corrugated metal. There was no door, allowing the rear end of an old model car to show.

A corrugated metal roof had been extended between the garage roof and the near eaves on the house to make a second doorless garage or storage shed. The interior was too dark to see, but a discarded water heater stood in the open door.

"Mrs. Yee is lucky she doesn't have to go through this hurricane," Tiffany said, letting her eyes drift back to the Nakamura's well-tended yard.

The hurricane's first gusty winds started to tear at the palms and the blossoms of Hawaii's state flower, the hibiscus. The 30-foot-tall mango, its oval fruit dangling on the end of foot-long cords, began swinging like a pendulum. Overhead, electric wires danced to a wild tune, and bits of debris skittered down the empty street.

"The hurricane's starting," Tiffany said. "We'd better go join Mom and Mrs. Nakamura."

"I want to stay and watch what happens," Nathan said.

"Mom won't let you. Come on."

Reluctantly, the boy followed her across the living room. "Do you think Mrs. Yee's house will blow down?"

"Let's hope not," Tiffany answered, her thoughts leaping to her father, Josh, and Dr. Nakamura. *If the hurricane could blow down trees and houses, what's it going to do to them, out there in the swamp?*

***

In the shack Josh stared at Franks, who stood between him and the door. The big man raised his voice to be heard above the noise of the hurricane starting to hurl itself against the metal cabin.

"Kid, you're not going anywhere until you tell me where you got this map."

Josh looked about wildly for some other way to escape, but there was no window or other opening of any kind besides the door. Still, he started backing until he almost fell backwards over the pile of rope.

Garcia warned, "Josh, you'd better tell him. He's a mean one when he's riled up."

Slowly, Josh nodded. "I found it on the floor of the helicopter."

"You're a liar!" Franks yelled, shaking the map in front of the boy's face. "You stole this from me!"

Josh vigorously shook his head. "No, I didn't! I found it just . . ."

He broke off his protest upon hearing voices outside the

door. Josh blurted, "That's Tank and the others!" He reached to open the door.

Franks blocked the way. "You 'n' me ain't through, kid," he said, hard eyes boring into Josh's. "I want to know more about that map."

Garcia protested, "Franks, that'll have to wait! You can't leave those people outside in this storm!"

"Don't tell me what I have to do!" Franks growled at his companion, but opened the door. It was jerked from his hands as the force of the wind caught it.

Malama was practically blown through the opening, followed by Tank, the pilot, Eddie, Miha, and the dog. All four men were needed to slowly close the door against the winds. Then they dragged the cots over and braced it.

Josh leaned weakly against the door, feeling the wind continue to assault it. The interior was now in deep gloom as though it was twilight instead of midday.

"Whew!" Josh cried, smiling at the newcomers. They were all thoroughly soaked. "I'm sure glad to see all of you." He wanted to explain what had happened with the map, but this wasn't the time.

Franks said sarcastically to Keegan and Eddie, "I see you didn't make it to the cave."

Josh swallowed hard, realizing that they could have if it hadn't been for him. He started to say he was sorry, but Eddie spoke first.

"We were concerned about Josh and came to check on him."

The little shack trembled as another, more powerful gust of wind assaulted it. Josh glanced helplessly at those who had come to look for him, filled with anguish at what his delay had caused.

***

The portable radio was on as Tiffany and Nathan entered the Nakamura kitchen. The announcer said, "The National Weather Service reports that Iniki's worst impact will likely come between four and six o'clock. It will bring torrential rains and sustained winds."

Mrs. Nakamura turned the set down. "I think we've done all we can, so we may as well go to our safe place."

"Mom," Nathan spoke up. "Can I stay and look outside for awhile?"

His mother glanced at Mrs. Nakamura, who sighed. "Our boys were still home when Hurricane Iwa hit us. I let them watch for a few minutes. I think it's safe this early in the storm."

Mrs. Ladd nodded to her son. "All right, for five minutes. But stay back from the windows and come when I call. Understand?"

With a joyful whoop, Nathan headed for the living room.

Tiffany started to follow, but her mother stopped her. "May I please speak to you alone?"

A cold chill of anxiety swept over Tiffany. She recognized that her mother's tone of voice meant trouble.

Nathan sensed it too, because he stopped and looked at her.

Tiffany formed angry, silent words so that only he could see. "Did you tell her about Rusty?"

When he shook his head, she relaxed a little, but uneasily followed her mother into the bedroom where Tiffany had slept last night.

"Close the door, please."

When Tiffany had complied, her mother motioned for her to sit on the edge of the bed. Reluctantly, she obeyed, easing down on the box spring. Her mother stood before her, hands on hips.

"Tiffany," she began quietly, "a while ago I overheard something that concerns me. Did you tell some boy that you are 16 years old?"

Tiffany stormed silently at her secret being known, but reluctantly confessed. "Yes, Mom."

"Why?"

"It just sort of popped out."

"I'm really surprised, Tiffany. You were taught to tell the truth."

"It wasn't a big deal, Mom!" She stood up to face her mother with defiant eyes. "So I'm 14 instead of 16. Who cares?"

"I care." Mrs. Ladd's voice was very low and soft, yet there was strength in it. "Your father and I care very much. So I'd like to understand why you lied."

"It wasn't really a lie, Mom. I just stretched the truth a bit, you know — a little white lie."

"There are no shades in lying! An untruth is a lie, and you know it. Now, how did it happen?"

Having no choice, Tiffany told about the experience at Waikiki Beach with Ashley Crawford. "So when she said she was 16," Tiffany finished, "I did the same. It just sort of slipped out."

"I see. This boy, Rusty. How come you've never invited him over with your other friends?"

Because you and Dad wouldn't like him, that's why! The thought flared hotly in her mind, but Tiffany merely shrugged. "No reason, I guess."

"Perhaps you thought your father and I wouldn't approve of him."

Tiffany's temper flared. "Nobody likes him! Josh warned me. . . ." She stopped, biting off the words, but it was too late. She lowered her head, fighting angry tears.

Her mother walked over and gently lifted Tiffany's face. "Josh warned you about what?"

Knowing she was digging herself deeper and deeper into a hole, Tiffany pursed her lips, searching for the right words to say. When she couldn't, she said nothing.

"Did Josh and you quarrel, Tiffany?"

"I don't want to talk about it, Mom."

"Very well." Mrs. Ladd replied, reaching into her apron pocket.

Tiffany's eyes widened as her mother pulled out Rusty's chain with the five-pointed, star-shaped pendant. With an inward groan of anguish, Tiffany realized that her little brother had unknowingly dropped it.

"Do you know what this is, Tiffany?"

"No," she replied honestly.

"I didn't either when I found it on the hallway floor a few minutes ago. It wasn't there earlier. As I examined it, I remembered something that made me uneasy. I looked it up in Mrs. Nakamura's dictionary. It's a pentagram."

Pentagram! That's what Rusty called it, but I never could remember. Tiffany waited in fearful silence.

"It's used as an occult* symbol."

"The occult?" Tiffany's surprise showed.

"You didn't know that, did you, dear?"

"No."

"I know Mrs. Nakamura wouldn't have such a thing in her house, and Nathan never wears anything around his neck. However, I've noticed that some older boys, teenagers, sometimes do wear chains or pendants around their necks.

"And you wear various chains around your neck, like the one you now have on with the cross hanging from it. Does that cross have meaning to you, Tiffany?"

"Yes, of course."

"Do you think it's logical that this pentagram also has special meaning to the one who wore it?"

"I suppose."

"Do you know that this symbol stands for the opposite of your cross?"

"I . . . I never would have guessed," Tiffany replied, helpless to stop the question she knew was coming.

"Do you know whose this is, or how it got in this house?"

Wildly, Tiffany sought to avoid answering. "Mom, the hurricane's going to start any minute. . . ."

"Answer me, please!"

Tiffany forced herself to look her mother straight in the eye. "I don't know whose it is," she lied, "or how it got in here."

The hurricane's first furious gust of wind hurled itself against the house, making Tiffany jump.

"Very well," Mrs. Ladd replied, casting a quick glance out the taped window. "We'd better get to our safe place. But first, I'd like to say another prayer for your father, brother, and the others, wherever they are."

***

In the cramped six-by-ten-foot swamp shack, everyone sat on the floor, backs braced against the far wall away from the door. Josh had tried to sit by Tank, but Franks squeezed his big bulk in between. Garcia sat next to Josh on the other side.

They're trying to keep me from talking to Tank about the map, Josh decided. But that concern was nothing compared to the danger presented by the hurricane. Its intensity rose fearfully, developing into a frightening pattern of wind and rain that could only be heard and felt in the windowless structure.

Keegan, the helicopter pilot, said he estimated the wind to be well over 100 miles an hour. It slammed into the shack with ever-increasing intensity, screamed under the roof and tried to pry it up. Josh and the others looked up fearfully at the scary sound of nails being pulled loose, warning that the roof could be blown away.

Each powerful gust passed, to be followed by a moment of quiet. Then the whole pattern was repeated, but with rising intensity.

To this was added the rain, which fell so hard on the corrugated metal roof that it seemed a thousand drummers in a marching band could not have made such a racket. The combined noise of wind and rain made Josh think of countless heavy jet planes all trying to land on the tiny cabin. And the hurricane had just begun.

Josh was greatly relieved to be with Tank, Keegan, Eddie, his daughter, and the dog. But he was also sick at heart, knowing he had caused them to be prisoners of the storm in this rickety old shelter instead of being safe in the cave.

Tank shouted loudly enough to be heard above the storm's fury. "Josh, I was hoping that you'd find your father and Dr. Nakamura in this shack."

"Me too." He cringed as another mighty blast of wind shook the shack, and broken limbs from the big ohia tree clattered on the metal roof. The building trembled, creaked and groaned.

Tank cried in alarm, "The whole place is going to blow away with us in it!"

"Easy, Tank!" Josh cautioned, reaching across Franks' big

body to touch his friend comfortingly on the forearm. "It'll be all right."

But Josh wasn't at all sure of that as another tremendous blast of wind smacked into the cabin, and the ripping sound of nails continued overhead.

He tried to shift his mind away from his own danger by thinking of his father and Dr. Nakamura somewhere out there in that hurricane. His thoughts leaped to his mother, sister and brother in Lihue.

They should be safe, Josh thought, *but are they?*

Chapter Ten

STORM OF THE CENTURY

When her mother's brief, impassioned prayer ended, Tiffany started to follow her from the bedroom, but stopped to look back as something smacked against the window crisscrossed with tape. She glimpsed a strip of asphalt roofing just before it was whipped off by the gusting winds.

The hurricane had just started, but the window was already moving in and out as the wind gusts passed. Tiffany was reminded of a human chest, rising and falling. At the same time, rain seeped in around the window's edges.

"Hurry up, please!" her mother urged. "Let's get away from that window before it blows in."

Greatly relieved to have her mother's questioning ended, Tiffany followed, but her conscience silently screamed at her. *You lied to your mother! You told her that you'd never seen that pentagram before. You lied to her just as you did to Rusty that day on the beach.*

Other accusing thoughts stung her mind, making her

squirm. *Those lies are starting to stack up! And with this one, you even looked your mother right in the eye. What's the matter with you?*

Tiffany was barely aware that her little brother was standing several feet back from the living room picture window, watching in fascination through the taped X.

"Mom! Tiffany! Look!"

"It's time to go to our safe place, Nathan," his mother said firmly.

"In just a sec, Mom! Tiffany, come see this!"

She glanced past her brother and through the window. The storm was fearful yet fascinating. Flying debris reminded her of big birds tumbling out of control. A huge piece of battered tin roofing from a carport skittered down the deserted street.

Asphalt shingles from some neighbor's house sailed by, wrapping themselves around a wooden power pole. Lights in the Nakamura house snapped off as utility lines fell. The house plunged into darkness in the middle of the day.

"Tiffany! Nathan! Come away from there."

They both began to back slowly toward their mother with their eyes still focused on the destruction taking place outside. A palm frond from the front yard tree ripped off of the wildly thrashing top.

The plumeria and hibiscus shrubs writhed in the gusting wind, their blossoms torn away. Limbs on the mango tree swayed to the hurricane's rhythm, the pace ever increasing.

"I want you two children to come now!"

Tiffany seemed not to hear her mother's voice. She kept

backing, but could not tear her eyes off of the most incredible sight she had ever seen.

The torrential rain, driven by 125-mile-an-hour winds, did not fall straight down. It was whipped sideways down the street in nearly solid sheets that were hard to see through.

Suddenly, Tiffany stiffened and pointed. "Mom, look! The Yee's place! It's going!"

"Wow!" Nathan cried. "Mom, you've got to see this!"

Tiffany heard her mother's quick step behind as she moved to where she could see across the street.

Tiffany held her breath as the hurricane's invisible fingers probed the Yee's house, shed, and garage, seeking entry and destruction. "Look, Mom! Look!"

The violent winds ripped the corrugated metal roof from the shed connecting the house to the garage. A piece of metal sheeting tumbled end-over-end into the air higher than the power poles. Then, like a stricken kite, the sheeting flopped clumsily across the electric lines.

The garage seemed to explode, showering pieces of boards and two-by-fours in all directions. The walls collapsed inwardly, partially crushing the parked car.

As the family groaned at the first destruction, the winds launched a fresh assault on the Yees' house. The roof's near end started to lift. It moved up an inch or so, then settled down, only to repeat the process as though some giant, invisible hands were getting a better, stronger grip.

"It's going!" Tiffany whispered hoarsely. "There!"

The end of the roof lifted several inches, then a foot. The

entire left side, perhaps 50 feet in length, suddenly tilted straight up. It hesitated in midair, then was hurled heavily to the left to fall in the yard.

A split second later, the right side also lifted high above the house, then fell straight back, out of sight behind the now roof-less dwelling.

"Wow!" Nathan exclaimed "It's all gone already!"

"It's awful!" Tiffany replied, turning to her mother. "It's so awful!"

Mrs. Ladd took both children by the hand and led them away. "And we can't do a thing about it. I've never felt so helpless."

Nathan asked plaintively, "Could this house get blown away, too?"

"I don't think so. This is much newer and probably much better made."

Tiffany's thoughts played leapfrog. "If the hurricane could do that to the Yees' place at the start of the storm, what chance could Dad and Josh possibly have out there in the swamp?"

"All we can do is trust that God will help them," Mrs. Ladd answered quietly.

They entered the kitchen, where Mrs. Nakamura picked up the portable radio. Together, they made their way down the hallway while the wind gusts whistled under the eaves, shook the house and promised much worse to come.

***

In the swamp the first few hours had passed with the shack somehow holding together. But the awesome gusts of wind had loosened one corner of the roof just enough so that a piece of the dark afternoon clouds could be seen along with the rain that seeped in.

Josh asked Eddie, "When will the eye of the hurricane come so we can go on to the cave?"

He shrugged. "Maybe four, five hours."

Garcia leaped up with a frenzied screech. "Four or five hours? I can't stand this for that long!"

"Shut up!" Franks said, pulling the little man down to the floor again. "Get a grip on yourself."

"I can't! The pressure on my ears is killing me! It's so hot I'm suffocating. I've got to get out. . . ."

He left his sentence incomplete, jerked away from his companion and rushed toward the door.

Eddie leaped up. "Don't open that door! We could all get sucked out. . . ."

He broke off as Keegan, sitting nearer the door, stretched out his foot and tripped the frantic man, who crashed face first onto the floor.

"Sorry, Garcia," the pilot said, helping him to his feet. "Are you hurt?"

The little man shook his head and pulled his long neck protectively into his shoulders.

With all eyes on Garcia, Josh found his first opportunity to speak privately to Tank. He leaned close to Tank and spoke in a loud whisper that wasn't heard above the hurricane's thunderous fury. "Franks got the map back."

"He did? How?"

"Fell out of my pocket when he and Garcia came in."

"Now what?"

Josh shook his head. "I don't know."

He couldn't say anything more because Keegan and Franks brought the whimpering Garcia back and eased him down against the wall. He had a small bump on his forehead.

"I'm scared, too," Josh said, trying to comfort the man. "But I have faith that we'll make it."

"Faith?" Garcia asked with a frown.

Josh looked up, but he wasn't seeing the roof that threatened to be blown off. He looked beyond the hurricane's dark clouds. "Faith in God," he said.

Franks laughed. "Next thing you know, Garcia, the kid will have you praying."

The pilot said bluntly, "Franks, leave them alone."

Garcia extended his long neck like a turtle venturing in trust from its shell. "How do you have this faith, Josh?"

How do I? Josh hurriedly asked himself. *And how do I share that with Mr. Garcia?*

The boy took a deep breath and began. "Well, my father says that there comes a time in everybody's life when we all need something or Someone bigger than ourselves.

"So you just have to believe there is Someone like that. My parents started teaching me about the Lord when I was little.

They'd already taught my older sister. Later, they taught my little brother.

"They're not here, but I have what I learned. Right now, faith is all we have."

Franks snorted. "Faith's not going to keep this place from blowing apart. It'll be pure luck if we live to get out of here and to the cave when the eye passes."

Keegan said bluntly, "Leave them alone, Franks."

The big poacher fell silent while the hurricane raged on.

***

At that moment, Mrs. Ladd, Tiffany, and Nathan sat under a king-size mattress in the Nakamura's bedroom listening to a portable radio. The announcer had earlier said that they were on emergency generator power because all the electricity was out across the island.

He continued, "While we're waiting for the next update from authorities, here's a brief recap of events thus far.

"By 10 A.M., winds were already beginning to bear down on Kauai, forewarning of the incredibly more-powerful forces to come. At 10:30 A.M., authorities ordered everyone off the streets.

"At 11 A.M., 80-mile-an-hour winds were recorded and civil defense sirens sounded their final doleful warning. At 1:30, monstrous winds were assaulting the island, but there have been reports of a few foolhardy people still outside.

"The eye of the storm is expected to pass directly over the center of Kauai about 3 P.M. Authorities warn against being fooled by this sudden quiet, for the hurricane will resume, perhaps with even more fury, until roughly 5 P.M. Then it should . . ."

Tiffany mentally tuned out, thinking to herself, *It's going to be a long, dangerous day.*

It was incredibly hot under the mattress shelter, especially with Tiffany, Nathan, their mother, and Mrs. Nakamura squeezed into such cramped quarters.

Tiffany tried to force her mind away from the sound of things being blown against the side of the house and of items falling off walls somewhere in the house. She didn't want to think about the possibility of the roof blowing off, or the sliding glass door or picture window exploding in the powerful gusting winds.

Yet all those thoughts nibbled at her, along with concern for her father and brother.

Now there was a new one: the lie she had told her mother about Rusty's pentagram. She could blame Josh for the quarrel they'd had, but she could blame no one but herself for the bold-faced lie she had told her mother.

She silently agonized over this during the first couple of hours while the storm intensified. The wind came in gusts, with indescribable noise levels far beyond anything Tiffany had ever heard before.

Rain fell so heavily that it was far beyond any drumming on a roof. This was like a giant gone mad, beating with war clubs on every inch of the house.

Tiffany's thoughts were suddenly shattered by a new and more fearsome sound. "Listen!" she exclaimed. "What's that?"

Mrs. Nakamura looked up and said quietly, "Those are big nails being pulled out of the wood."

"From the roof?" Nathan cried in disbelief.

Mrs. Nakamura nodded, licking her lips, but saying nothing more.

Alarmed, Tiffany stuck her head out from under the overhead mattress. Her eyes widened in horror. Ceiling plaster fell heavily to the floor, and Tiffany could see into the attic. Through the wooden trusses, she saw that a corner of the roof had torn loose. Rain whipped in. The glowering sky was visible beyond.

"Mom!" she screamed, ducking back under the shelter. "The roof's going!"

Mrs. Nakamura spoke first. "Quickly, everyone, grab your things and run to the hall closet! Hurry! Hurry!"

Tiffany was so badly frightened that later she didn't remember snatching up the portable radio, a flashlight, and a plastic jug of bottled water. She squeezed into the closet with the others and pulled the door shut.

Mrs. Nakamura urged, "Make yourselves as comfortable as possible. If the roof goes, and even most of the house, this closet is the one place most likely to still remain standing. And there are no windows, so we don't have to worry about glass blowing in on us."

The electricity was still off, so only flashlights provided any illumination as Tiffany tried to still her racing heart. Earlier, the closet had seemed large enough, but now it was suffocatingly small.

They all sat on the floor, their backs against the wall. Tiffany joined the others in fearfully listening to hear if the entire roof would be ripped off.

"Blankets!" Mrs. Nakamura quickly passed around those she had earlier stacked in the closet. Above the fearsome howling of the wind, she explained, "If the roof goes, the rain will beat straight down on us. It'll be miserable, but these blankets will help some."

The four fugitives from the storm added to their already hot, uncomfortable situation by huddling under the blankets.

No one spoke as they concentrated on listening to the sound of more nails being ripped violently from their places. But terror came from another direction.

An explosive sound of glass breaking made Tiffany jump and look questioningly at the women.

Mrs. Nakamura said, "That was the sliding glass door in our . . ."

Tiffany didn't hear any more. Something stabbed her right shoulder, causing great pain. She started to leap up, then saw in the gloom that a trickle of blood was flowing from her little brother's scalp.

Tiffany twisted around to look behind them. Shards of glass were stuck through the wallboard. Gaping holes showed where other shrapnel-like pieces had penetrated.

It was obvious that the wind had driven pieces of the broken glass door through the wall and into her back.

Mrs. Ladd seemed to grasp the situation instantly. "How badly are you hurt?" she cried. "Here, let me see."

Tiffany felt blood running down her shoulder blade.

"We're going to die!" Nathan shrieked. "We're all going to die!"

Chapter Eleven

INTO THE HURRICANE'S EYE

Mrs. Ladd took a firm hold on her young son who was still repeating, "We're going to die!"

"Nathan, don't say that!" she exclaimed. She picked up a two-cell flashlight and turned it on. "Here, let me see your scalp."

He sniffled as she quickly examined his wound.

"It's nothing serious," she decided. "Paula, would you please open the first aid kit? He'll feel better with some antiseptic and a bandage. Thanks. Now, Tiffany, turn around and let me see what's happened."

Tiffany obeyed, moving so that her mother could shine the flashlight on the wound. Tiffany was fearful because she could feel blood. "How bad is it?"

"There's just a little piece of glass sticking in your shoulder. Hold still. I'll pull it out."

Tiffany flinched as the shard was removed. Her mother held the piece where Tiffany could see it. Barely half an inch long, the glass had blood only on the point.

Her mother wiped the blood away, and applied antiseptic and a bandage while Tiffany's fears gradually lessened.

She became aware of the wind screaming down the hallway from the broken sliding door in the master bedroom. Sounds of others things being thrown about the house marked the wind's passage through the building.

Greatly relieved that she hadn't been seriously injured, Tiffany said, "Oh, Mrs. Nakamura, I'm so sorry! Your house will be a total wreck."

There were tears in Mrs. Nakamura's eyes when she answered softly, "Thank you. Such things can be replaced. I'm just glad that we're all still alive."

"But it's not over!" Nathan said, gingerly touching his bandaged scalp.

"It may just be wishful thinking on my part," Mrs. Nakamura replied, "but I do believe it's calming down a little outside. Notice how the wind isn't gusting so hard? I think the rain is easing up somewhat too. Maybe the eye of the hurricane is coming."

In another half hour, a strange calm announced that the eye of the hurricane was directly overhead. When Mrs. Nakamura felt it was safe, she gingerly opened the closet door and stepped into the hall.

"Oh, my!" Mrs. Ladd cried in dismay.

Tiffany had never seen such a mess. Everything that could be blown out of the master bedroom was scattered along the hallway. Broken glass was everywhere.

The living room was worse. The floor, which she had vacuumed before the hurricane, was now littered with papers, magazines, books, and pieces of glass.

Tiffany was surprised to see that the large picture window was still intact. *Guess I did a good job taping that* she told herself with pride.

Mrs. Nakamura led her guests outside. She tilted her face toward the sky. "Last time," she commented, "during Hurricane Iwa, there was no rain when the eye was overhead. It was clear, and we could see blue sky straight up. We could even see the outline of the eye itself. But not now. It's still overcast and drizzling."

Tiffany stared in awe at what the first part of the hurricane had done. The wind had blown every flower and most of the leaves off the plumeria and other plants.

The stately mango tree was denuded of leaves, and broken limbs littered the ground. Palm fronds and pieces of cardboard and metal cluttered the once-neat lawn.

The street was impassable because of fallen utility poles and a snake's nest of downed wires. Across the street, there was only rubble where the Yee house had stood.

"Oh, that poor woman!" Mrs. Ladd exclaimed. "She has nothing left!"

"She has her life," Mrs. Nakamura replied. "I know her. When she returns from the Mainland, she'll rebuild."

Other neighbors ventured outdoors, calling to each other. Mr. Park, the Nakamura's closest neighbor, called, "Everyone all right?"

When assured they were, he called back, "Us, too, but we lost some roofing. I hope we don't lose the whole thing."

"Same here," Mrs. Nakamura replied. She led the others around to inspect the damage and announced that it could have been worse. "Let's check on the bedroom," she said.

Tiffany's mother headed toward the kitchen. "The rest of you go ahead. I'm going to try phoning the helicopter people again."

At the master bedroom door, Tiffany sucked in her breath. The large sliding glass door was gone, leaving a gaping hole with jagged edges of glass in the frame.

The king-size mattress, which had been so awkward and heavy to move off the bed for a shelter, had been thrown across the room. It leaned upright against the wall. Bedding and furniture lay strewn about.

Tiffany exclaimed, "Oh, Mrs. Nakamura! How awful!"

"It's not pretty," she admitted, "but such things can be replaced. Our lives cannot. We have those, and that's what's really important."

"But the storm's not over, is it?" Tiffany asked.

"No, but the part that comes after the eye passes is usually shorter, although sometimes more violent."

"How short?" Nathan wanted to know.

"Oh, maybe an hour and a half."

Tiffany groaned. "That'll seem like forever."

They stood silently surveying the damage until Mrs. Ladd joined them. "I can't get through. Lines are down."

Tiffany sickened at the realization Josh and their father

could be dead, along with Tank and Dr. Nakamura. The last angry words Tiffany had spoken to Josh seared her memory.

She had considered herself a Christian since she was a little girl, so what she had said to Josh, and the lies she had told her mother, were against all Tiffany believed.

But now she was afraid of telling her mother the truth, and Josh might never be seen again. *Oh, I just wish I knew he was alive!*

***

Mighty gusts of wind continued to shake the swamp shack where another violent gust of wind tore at the loosened corner of the roof.

"There it goes!" Tank exclaimed as the corner started to sag under the weight of rain.

A piece of corrugated sheeting sailed away and the corner collapsed inward, causing everyone to scramble up and back as far away as possible.

"We're dead!" Garcia screamed. "We're all dead!"

"No, we're not!" the pilot cried. "The weight of the water on the roof caused that corner to collapse, but it'll soon drain off. Besides, I think I hear the storm easing off. So if that end of the roof holds up a little while longer, we can start for the cave."

Everyone except Garcia fell silent. He sank back down against the wall, closed his eyes and mumbled over and over, "Oh, God! Oh, God!"

It took a moment for Josh to realize that the man was praying in the only way he knew how.

Josh joined the others in listening hopefully as the rain and wind slowly faded away. Falling rain from the collapsed end of the roof eased off too, but there was so much water on the floor that everyone's feet were wet.

Finally, Eddie stood up. "The eye of the hurricane is almost here," he announced. "We'll have about fifteen minutes to reach the cave before the back side of the storm starts. . . ."

"I'm getting out of here now!" Franks interrupted, hoisting himself to his feet and pulling on his raincoat. One corner of the burlap sack still stuck out of one pocket. "Come on, Garcia. If you want to live through this thing, you've got to help yourself."

"Wait!" the pilot cried, but the big poacher yanked the door open and plunged through it.

The wind and rain gushed into the tiny room, making it rock so hard Josh feared it would blow off the foundation. The force of the wind made him turn his head momentarily. When he looked again, Franks and Garcia were gone, leaving their backpacks behind.

Eddie said sadly, "They shouldn't have done that."

A few minutes later, Eddie decided it was safe to head for the cave. Everyone stood and stepped outside.

Now only light rain fell, unlike the blinding downpour of the past few hours. The incredible gusting winds had completely died down. Josh squinted at the sky. The dark clouds warned that this was only a momentary lull. Greater natural fury was coming.

As one, Josh, Tank, and Malama joined the two men in looking at the cabin.

"Wow!" Tank exclaimed. "Would you look at that?"

The building tilted precariously. Much of the siding had been stripped away, leaving only the wooden parts. Broken tree limbs covered the roof except for the part the wind had raised. The ohia tree leaned dangerously over the cabin.

"Thank God it held together this long," Keegan said softly.

Josh glance at the pilot, then slowly nodded. "Yes, thank God."

"Fifteen minutes before the eye passes," Eddie warned. "We'd better be in the cave before then, or we may not be so lucky when the back side of the storm hits."

It was very hard going because the hillside was slick, and there were countless downed trees, uprooted shrubs and mud slides everywhere. Still, Josh was so glad to be out of the shack that he didn't really mind.

Maybe Dad and Dr. Nakamura are in the cave, Josh thought, ignoring the mud that weighted down his shoes. He hurried through the hurricane's eye in renewed hope.

***

About ten minutes after the eye of the hurricane arrived over Lihue, Mrs. Nakamura finished leading her guests on an inspection tour of the house. Only one small window had blown out, along with the large sliding glass door in the master bedroom. Wind rushing through the house had created a tremendous mess, but there was surprisingly little damage from rain that had also blown in.

"It's bad," she admitted sadly. "But the roof hasn't blown off, so it's not hopeless."

Suddenly, Tiffany stiffened in alarm. "Listen! What's that?"

"Sounds exactly like a freight train coming," her mother replied. "But there are no trains here."

"The eye has passed," Mrs. Nakamura announced. "The wind has changed direction, and the hurricane is starting again. Quick, back to the closet!"

Everyone had barely settled into their safe place when Tiffany heard the terrifying sound rushing upon them. This wind was different from what had come before the hurricane's eye. That wind had come in powerful and fearsome gusts from the right, but hadn't howled except around the eaves of the house. But since the wind had changed direction toward the left, it had taken on a whole new sound.

Tiffany and the others had just entered the closet and closed the door when the first gust hit. The house rocked so hard that Nathan yelled in pure terror.

"Earthquake! Earthquake!"

"No, it's just the wind!" Mrs. Nakamura replied, joining the boy's mother in reassuring him.

Tiffany fought down panic as the wind rumbled away, fading into the distance like a passing train. Slowly, she started to relax.

Nathan cried, "Here it comes again!"

The rumbling began in the distance, then roared toward the house as before. "Hang on!" Tiffany cried.

The house again shook with the fury of the wind. Tiffany heard more nails being violently yanked loose. She wondered how long before the whole roof flew off.

An hour of mental anguish dragged by, an hour of rumbling wind, of earthquake forces shaking the house, then fading in the distance to the right, only to come rumbling again from the left.

"I can't stand this!" Nathan shouted as the hurricane continued unabated. "I have to get out of here! We're all going to die if we stay."

"Nathan, don't panic!" His mother reached to grab him, but he nimbly leaped up, grabbed the closet door and leaped into the hallway.

"I'll get him!" Tiffany exclaimed, springing to her feet and dashing down the hall. Wind pouring through the shattered master bedroom door almost knocked her off her feet. "Nathan, stop!" she cried.

He disappeared into the bedroom where he had slept last night. Tiffany followed. He had thrown himself on the box spring and pulled a pillow over his head.

"Nathan, please," she said, softening her voice when she wanted to angrily yell at him. "I'm scared too, but it's going to be all right."

He didn't answer, but his body shook with frightened sobs. She sat beside him and gently removed the pillow. "Come on, Nathan. It's safer back in the closet."

"No! I'll die in there!"

She gently pulled him into her arms, speaking soft words of encouragement and hope even though her own fears made her heart race.

Her eyes drifted to the window. The glass still held, crisscrossed with tape she and Nathan had hurriedly put there. Wind forced rain to seep in around the edges. Her gaze went through the window to the next-door neighbor's house.

She leaped to her feet with a shriek. "Mr. Park's roof!" she gasped. "Look! Look!"

Nathan sat up and looked just as the hurricane forces pried up the far end of the roof, then let it down. At once, it rose again, hesitated, then settled back down. As it started up the third time, Tiffany acted.

"Run!" she screamed, grabbing Nathan's wrist and practically jerking him off the bed.

She was almost to the door with Nathan stumbling after her when she glanced back. She caught only a glimpse of the neighbor's entire roof lifting free, then hurtling in one piece through the air, headed straight for the Nakamura's home.

Tiffany tried to open the door and shove Nathan into the hallway, but it was too late. With an incredible noise of breaking timbers and glass, the flying roof crashed through the bedroom window, tearing out the entire wall.

Tiffany threw herself protectively across her little brother just as the room collapsed, trapping them both under the wreckage!

Chapter Twelve

A QUESTION OF LIFE OR DEATH

Tiffany opened her eyes but couldn't see anything. She heard the hurricane's furious wind and rain inches away. Then she remembered what had happened. Her heart drummed harder, and she had trouble breathing.

Her little brother groaned, and Tiffany rolled off him. She gasped when her insides exploded with pain.

Nathan asked, "What happened?"

Fighting to keep from fainting, Tiffany gingerly sat up and forced herself to answer calmly. "The neighbor's roof blew off and smashed into our house. We must be underneath it. Are you hurt?"

"I . . . I don't know." He hesitated, then added plaintively, "But I'm scared, Tiffany!"

"Me too," she admitted, quickly running her hands over him in the darkness, feeling for blood or broken bones while her own body silently screamed with its injuries. "I think you're okay," she said with relief.

"I wish we could see better."

Tiffany could barely discern him in their tiny prison. "I do too. But for now, let's try to get out of here."

A quick examination by touch convinced her that they were in a cramped area about four feet high, five feet wide, and five feet long.

"I think we're under the point of Mr. Park's roof," she decided. "It feels like the floor of your bedroom under us where the roof and house smashed together."

"Can we get out?" Nathan's voice held panic.

"I can't feel any way, but don't worry. Mom will find somebody to get us out."

"When?"

"When?" Tiffany repeated the word, trying to think clearly while her body screamed with pain. "Pretty soon."

"My head hurts."

She felt it in the darkness and gulped upon touching a large bump. *I wonder if he has a concussion?* She tried to remember her first aid course, then felt around his ears. She stopped with a frightened gulp when her fingers felt blood. *Bad sign!*

"Will I live?" Nathan asked plaintively.

Her automatic reaction was to assure him that he would, but the searing pain inside her body, and the mental anguish of the lies she'd told stopped her.

"I hope so, but I don't really know," she said honestly.

***

In the lull of the hurricane's eye, Josh gasped for breath as he followed single file behind Eddie and the group heading for the cave. The exertion of pulling his feet out of ankle-deep muck each step was compounded by the danger of not reaching shelter before the storm started up again.

"How much farther?" Josh asked as the party rounded the base of a small mountain.

"A few minutes," Eddie replied. "The cave's just around that next bend."

Malama stopped in the mud, her breath coming in rasping sounds. "Dad, I'm sorry, but I've got to rest and catch my breath."

"Same here," the pilot said, stopping with Eddie and the dog. "I've never seen such hard walking."

Eddie announced, "We'd better all take a breather. No sense in causing a heart attack or something."

Everyone else stopped, but Josh was too anxious to do that. "I'll go on ahead. I have to see if my dad's in that cave. You coming, Tank?"

He groaned but nodded. "Okay, if I stand here, I might sink into the mud so deep I'd never get out."

Josh smiled in appreciation at his friend as they continued through the light rain.

Eddie warned, "Be careful, boys! Some wild pigs or dogs might have taken shelter in that cave."

"We will," Josh promised, hurrying as fast as he could with Tank beside him. Soon they came to an ancient lava ridge where the mud wasn't so deep. The boys made better time, leaving the others behind.

Upon rounding the bend, Josh spotted the entrance to the cave. It was about five feet wide and as high. Countless rivulets of rain water poured down the mountainside to cascade over the opening. Rocks, tree limbs, and other debris swept along with the water also fell across the cave's mouth. A small stream of water plunged off the overhead lip and flowed into the interior darkness.

Josh forced himself to jog forward, eager to see if his father and Dr. Nakamura were in the cave.

Near the entrance Tank stopped abruptly and glanced off to one side. "Pig tracks," he whispered, pointing at the fresh prints in the mud. "Big ones, too!"

"I don't think so. These are too wide for pigs, so these must have been made by swamp goats with the splayed hooves we heard about. Anyway, the tracks lead away from the cave, so they're gone."

As he started forward again, Tank muttered, "Let's hope the pigs are too. And that there are no wild dogs."

A few steps farther, Josh stopped and looked down. "Boot prints!" he exclaimed. They began at the cave's mouth and disappeared down the hill. "These were made after the rain stopped, or they'd be washed away by now."

"A big man made those," Tank observed.

"Maybe my dad. He's over six feet tall, so they're probably his." He moved on again.

Tank grabbed his arm. "Wait! Franks could also have made these prints!"

"If he did, where are Garcia's tracks?"

"Hmm? Well, if your dad made these, where are Dr. Nakamura's tracks?"

"Maybe he's still inside the cave."

"Or maybe it's Garcia in there."

"It just *has* to be my dad. Come on, let's find out."

Just outside the entrance, the boys bent their heads to step inside. Then they straightened up because the ceiling was about seven feet high.

Josh peered around cautiously, smelling the faint, unpleasant odor of dampness and mildew. The cave was hot, dark, and gloomy, but not very deep. He could make out the back wall twelve feet away from the entrance. To the right, he could see the side wall ten feet away. He could not make out the left wall through the soft darkness.

"Hear anything?" Josh asked.

"No, but my breathing's so loud, and my heart is pounding so hard from walking in this mud that I can barely hear you."

Josh stepped around the stream of water pouring through the right side of the cave's mouth.

"We'll drown in there," Tank warned.

"I don't think so. Most of the floor looks dry. The rain is pouring into the cave from off the mountain, but see how the cave floor slopes down toward the back wall? The water isn't backing up, so it must be draining out somewhere inside." He paused, following the water across the floor to where it had collected in a small pool against the back wall.

"Yes. Hear that gurgling sound? That means the water is draining out through a hole in the floor near the back wall. Let's keep going."

Cautiously, Josh took a couple of steps onto the dry volcanic rock and dirt floor while his eyes adjusted to the cave's interior. He suspiciously eyed the soft darkness and silence to his left. *I wonder how far it goes?*

He stopped and called. "Anybody in here?"

There was no answer. He took a step forward. Something struck his shoe top. *Snake!* he thought in panic, forgetting that there are none on Kauai. He fearfully glanced down.

Tank laughed. "A frog!"

"Big green one!" Josh tipped his shoe so it slid off. "Lots of them. Came in out of the hurricane."

He moved carefully to avoid stepping on the others as they hopped heavily out of the way. "I wish we could see the end of this part of the cave."

"If somebody's in here, why doesn't he answer?" Tank added hastily, as if answering his own question. "Unless it's Garcia. He could be waiting to . . ."

"Shh!" Josh interrupted, stopping abruptly. "I think I heard something." He strained to see through the dim light. "Yes, there *is* somebody over there!"

"It's probably Garcia! Let's wait for the others."

"Hello?" Josh called. "Anybody in here?"

His voice echoed around the cave.

"Who's . . . there?" The words were slow and halting.

Josh turned to Tank. "That's not Franks or Garcia."

"Then it must be . . ."

"Dr. Nakamura?" Josh interrupted with another call. He headed to his left. "Is that you?"

"Yes. Who are you?"

"Josh. John Ladd's son. And my friend, Tank Catlett." Josh hurried toward the sound of the voice until he made out the dark shadow of a man sitting against the far wall about twenty feet from the entrance. "Are you okay?"

"My . . . ankle." He paused as the boys approached. "Josh, you said?" The ornithologist's voice was weak. "Yes, I remember now. John's son. And Tank. I've heard about you two."

Josh and Tank dropped to their knees beside Dr. Nakamura. By the faint light from outside, Josh saw that the man's clothes were soaked. Black hair streaked with gray hung in wet strands over his brown eyes. His face was pale and twisted with pain. His left boot and sock had been removed, revealing a badly swollen ankle.

"I must have passed out," Dr. Nakamura continued. "I came to when I heard your voices. I thought you were those men. . . ."

"What men?" Josh asked, fearing the answer.

"The same ones your father and I saw leaving our camp shortly after dawn. We were returning after again looking for the birds when we saw those strangers."

Tank asked, "What did they look like?"

"One was big, like John. The other was much shorter. We

thought they'd robbed us, so we chased them. But they got away when I fell. . . ."

"Franks and Garcia!" Tank broke in.

Josh nodded to Tank, then turned to Dr. Nakamura. "Where's my dad?"

"He just went to get our backpacks. After I hurt myself, we had to leave them so John could help me hobble here. The hurricane struck just before . . ." He winced in pain and didn't finish his sentence.

Josh asked, "Could we take a look at your ankle?"

"Thanks, but John already did. He thinks it's just a sprain. There's a first aid kit in my backpack. John went for that, and some food. We only had an apple and two candy bars in our pockets, and nothing to treat this ankle."

"I'll go see if I can find my dad," Josh said.

"No!" Dr. Nakamura spoke sharply. "You'll get lost. He's got a map. . . ."

"Not anymore," Josh interrupted. He added ruefully, "Those two men have it." He quickly explained.

The ornithologist commented, "That's why they sneaked into our camp—to steal my map. They probably planned to use it later in trapping the birds. So they took the map and were headed back to civilization when your helicopter found them."

Josh's thoughts were with his father. He asked, "How far did my dad have to go for your backpacks?"

"Not far," Dr. Nakamura replied. "It's down by a little stream. Well, by now it's probably as wide and deep as the Mississippi."

Tank observed, "That must be the stream we crossed before getting to the shack."

"Has to be," Josh agreed. "Dr. Nakamura, I know where that is, so I'll go meet my dad."

"No need to do that, Josh. He'll be back soon."

"But what if something happens to him, all alone out . . ."

A dog's bark interrupted Josh. He turned to see Kahu enter the cave ahead of Keegan, Eddie, and Malama.

"We found Dr. Nakamura," Josh told them. He quickly added details of what the ornithologist had told him.

"I've got a first aid kit," Eddie said, slipping the pack from his back. Josh introduced the ornithologist to the new arrivals as all three bent over the slumped figure.

After they had shaken hands, Eddie opened his backpack. "I've got an elastic bandage in here. If that is just a sprain and not a break, this will help."

"So would an ice pack," the pilot said grimly. "That would help keep the swelling down."

The ornithologist forced a smile. "It's so sweltering in here that even if we had one, the ice would melt before you could even apply it to my ankle."

Unable to help, Josh walked back toward the mouth of the cave and stood hopefully looking out. The rain started to fall harder again, and the wind gusted.

Tank joined him, saying, "The eye is passing."

Josh sighed, feeling sick inside. "Something must have happened to Dad, or he'd be back by now."

"He'll probably be here any second."

Josh nodded, noticing that the wind had shifted direction. It caught the falling rain and whipped it sideways, driving a liquid sheet across the cave's mouth. Shielding his eyes for one final look for his father, Josh followed Tank back toward the other people on the left side of the cave.

Suddenly he spun around at a strange sound. He was startled to see a big brown billy goat and two larger black females in the entrance. They halted, apparently smelling the dog or the people. For a moment, they hesitated on splayed hooves. Their wet coats smelled awful.

Josh heard Kahu growl and saw him start toward the animals. The big male goat flattened his ears tight against his head and turned to meet the dog with lowered horns.

"Kahu, no!" Eddie spoke sharply. "Come here."

The dog obeyed. The brown goat shifted nervously, as if to leave, but a sudden violent gust of wind whipped his shaggy coat. He hesitated between the other goats, sniffing the air and snorting nervously.

Tank whispered, "They can't make up their minds whether they're more afraid of us or the hurricane."

After a couple of minutes, as the storm's fury increased, the billy cautiously entered. The other two goats followed, stepping over the green frogs and the running water to huddle at the opposite end of the cave.

Tank said, "I hope no pigs or wild dogs come in."

Josh was startled when a bird flew into the cave with a distinctive whirring noise. Even in the gloom, he could see that it was crimson with black wings and tail.

Upon spotting the people, the bird turned toward the cave's mouth as though to fly out, but a gust of wind caught it and blew it backward.

"That's an apapane,*" Malama said softly from behind Josh. "It's quite common, but it'll die if it goes back into the storm."

The bird seemed to have come to the same conclusion. It circled around and landed in a wet heap by the goats.

"That's better," Malama commented.

"Sure is," Josh agreed. "It looks really beat. . . ."

He broke off as two other birds fluttered into the cave. Their heads, backs, wings, and tail were black. There were bright yellow feathers on the legs. Josh recognized them from color drawings he had seen.

"Hey!" he whispered as the birds flew erratically around the cave, sounding a *keet-keet* alarm. "They look like those rare . . ."

Dr. Nakamura interrupted with a startled exclamation from the back wall. "I can't believe it! That's a pair of Kauai 'o'o'a'a!"

Kahu barked sharply, leaped up, and charged toward the cave's entrance. Josh whirled away from the birds to see a big man silhouetted against the outside light.

"Dad!" Josh cried joyously, rushing forward.

Chapter Thirteen

HELPLESS WHILE WAITING

"**D**ad, oh. . . !" Josh interrupted himself and drew back in surprise, staring at the big man silhouetted in the cave's mouth. "Mr. Franks!"

The poacher plunged into the cave, followed by his shorter companion, Garcia. Water poured from their rain slickers.

"So," Franks said, "we meet again, huh, kid?" He loosened a forest-green backpack and slid it from his shoulders to the floor. "Where're your friends. . . ? Phew! Hey, kid, what's that stink?"

"My name is Josh. And that's a wet goat smell."

"It's sickening!" Franks looked to where the goats huddled together in the far end of the cave. "Let's drive them out."

"No, you can't do that!" Josh exclaimed.

"Don't tell me what to do!" Franks snapped angrily. He lunged toward the three goats, waving his big arms.

"Look out!" Josh warned as the brown billy whirled, lowered his horns and started to charge.

Franks stopped so suddenly that Josh almost laughed. Slowly, the poacher backed up, eyeing the goat which had stopped but watched with baleful eyes.

Franks commented, "I guess it wouldn't be right to throw them out in the hurricane."

"No," Josh replied, stifling his laughter. "It wouldn't."

"Well, kid," Franks commented as Kahu approached, growling softly. "I see the mutt made it, along with your other friends."

Malama softly called the dog back to her side.

Josh took another look out of the cave entrance in hopes of seeing his father. The wind blew on and across the cave's mouth, sending in some leaves and other debris to whirl around inside.

The rain was again falling so hard that Josh could not see anything outside. With a soft sigh, he turned to follow Franks and Garcia toward the left side of the cave. It was much darker since the hurricane's eye passed.

"We found Dr. Nakamura," Josh said, stepping forward quickly to watch the poachers' eyes.

Garcia twitched as though he'd received an electric shock, but Franks bent over the ornithologist. "Hi, Doc."

"I've seen you two before," Dr. Nakamura observed weakly from where he leaned against the wall. "John and I chased you out of our camp at dawn this morning."

Franks shrugged and shifted his gaze to the bandaged ankle. "Yeah, I remember. I saw you fall, Doc. Looks like you hurt yourself. Where's your big friend?"

"Please don't call me Doc. And my friend's name is John. Josh, there, is his son."

"I know about the kid, but where's his old man?"

An angry retort welled up in Josh, but Dr. Nakamura spoke first. "Don't be disrespectful!"

"Okay, okay," Franks replied. "But where is he?"

"John went out a while ago to look for something," Dr. Nakamura replied. "Didn't you see him?"

"Nope," Franks answered shortly.

Garcia looked at Josh. "I'm sorry."

"Thanks." Josh turned away.

Tank came up alongside him. "Your dad's probably found some place where he's safe."

Josh shook his head. "We both know there's no shelter out there. Besides, I know that Dad wouldn't have left Dr. Nakamura alone like this if he could help it."

Franks ordered, "Hey, Garcia, open that backpack we found and see if there's anything to eat in it."

Josh spun around, remembering that the poachers had left their packs in the cabin. "You found that backpack?"

"Yes. There was another one, too," Garcia explained, "but it had fallen into the stream and caught in a tree. We couldn't get to it."

Dr. Nakamura said, "Let me see this one."

"No you don't!" Franks growled. "We found it."

Keegan reached out and snatched the pack from the little man. "Dr. Nakamura said he wants to see this."

Franks started to protest, then shrugged.

"This is *mine*," the ornithologist said. "My name's inside the top flap. See for yourself."

Franks swore vehemently and reached for the pack, but the pilot blocked him.

"Simmer down," Keegan advised. "You're big, but I'm sure that Eddie and I could toss you and your friend out of here if we wanted to."

. Garcia protested, "I'm not in on this."

"You miserable coward!" Franks thundered at him.

Garcia cringed but said nothing.

Dr. Nakamura held the pack out to the girl. "Malama, there are some apples, trail mix, candy bars, and other food in here. Pick out what you like, then share the rest with all the others."

Josh realized he should have been hungry, but he wasn't. He wanted to look outside again in hopes of seeing his father. He followed the inside front cave wall to stay out of the wind blowing into the cave.

He moved slowly so that he would not disturb the goats, frogs, or birds at the far end of the cave. The wet birds had apparently settled down on the floor, but Josh couldn't see them because of the deep gloom.

The frogs were barely visible on the cave floor. The birds were totally out of sight, but the three goats watched the boy warily through the swirling leaves and other debris. Josh shielded himself against the wall as best he could and again peered around the edge of the cave's mouth into the blinding rain.

Tank came up alongside him. "You've done all you can. There's nothing to do now but wait and pray."

Josh nodded, staring morosely out, knowing that something had happened to his father. But what? Was he alive? If so, where? And no matter where it was, could he survive this back side of the hurricane?

Malama walked up carrying an apple. "I hope your father's safe, Josh."

"Thanks, but nothing out in the open could live through this, so unless he found shelter . . ."

"I'm sure he did," she interrupted.

Josh studied her face. She was serious. There was none of the light, bantering manner she'd had when they first met that morning before the hurricane.

"Thanks, Malama."

She gave him a brief smile and gently took his arm. "Dad says we've got another hour and a half or so before the hurricane passes. You had better come back here with the rest of us."

Josh followed her and Tank back to the corner where all the others sat along the cave wall. Josh paid little attention to their conversation. He sat in gloomy silence, thinking about his father.

It's so maddening to sit here, doing nothing, when I know he's out there someplace close by. He's probably hurt or sick or something. Otherwise, he'd have come back to the cave before the eye passed. But I can't do a thing to help him. I hate being so helpless!

Then Josh remembered his sister, and the way they had parted with her angry words. He closed his eyes, trying to blot out the memory. *I wonder what she's doing now?*

***

Under the crushed section of roof and bedroom, Tiffany lay gasping for breath. Perspiration covered her forehead, but it was more from pain than exertion.

For the past several minutes, she had felt around in the small prison that held her and Nathan. Part of her efforts were to find a way of escape, but another reason had been to keep her mind off of how serious her internal injuries could be.

They're bad, she had silently concluded. *But I mustn't let Nathan know. He's scared enough already.*

"Tiffany?"

"What?"

"Can you pray?"

She hesitated, aware that even in this terrible predicament, she had not done what was natural. It was a little like when she had done something really wrong and didn't want to face her parents, only this was much more difficult.

She tried to sidetrack her brother. "Why don't you do it for us?" she asked softly.

"Well, okay, I guess. And I'll pray for Dad and Josh, too, wherever they are."

***

In the cave, Josh felt uneasy about his sister. He couldn't explain it, but he was definitely uneasy about her. To a lesser extent, he fretted about his brother, mother, and Mrs. Nakamura. But thoughts of Tiffany tormented Josh. In desperation, he tuned in to the discussion going on around him.

Franks spoke to the ornithologist around a mouthful of candy bar. "So you're the one who found a pair of rare Hawaiian 'o'o birds."

Dr. Nakamura replied with some heat, "And you're the poacher who's been following me, trying to find them so you can steal them and sell them on the black market."

"Now, now," Franks said without rancor, "don't get yourself all worked up, Doc."

"I told you that I don't like being called that!"

"And I don't like being called a poacher."

"What would you call yourself?" Dr. Nakamura demanded with rising anger in his tone.

"I'm an entrepreneur," Franks answered with a pleased grin. "Yeah, that's what I am."

"You're a poacher, plain and simple, and poaching is illegal. But you'll never get those birds. Never!"

"Doc, I'm betting a hundred thousand dollars that I do," Franks replied. "I'll get that for your birds."

Garcia spoke up in a pleading tone. "Aw, Franks, let's change the subject. Okay?"

Josh didn't like quarrels. He said, "That's a good idea. Let's talk about something else."

Tank leaned over and whispered in Josh's ear. "I wonder what those two poachers would do if they knew the birds they want so much are right here in this cave?"

Josh shifted his eyes toward the far end of the cave. He couldn't see the pair of 'o'o'a'a in the semi-darkness, but he knew they were there with the frogs and the goats, waiting for the storm to pass.

"Don't even think about it," Josh whispered back. "There's no telling what kind of trouble would result if Franks and Garcia knew."

Josh halfheartedly listened to the conversation that developed between Dr. Nakamura, Eddie and Garcia. The ornithologist explained that disease, especially from mosquitoes accidentally introduced by Europeans in the 17th century, had killed off most of the native forest birds.

Eddie spoke of the various swamp and forest birds' eating habits, ranging from insects to nectar from the ohia blossoms. He told how yellow feathers used in the ancient Hawaiians' capes and helmets came from the thigh of the Kauai 'o'o. Each bird only had a couple of those.

"The red feathers," he continued, "mostly came from the 'i'iwi,* which is still fairly common. To a lesser extent, the apapane's crimson breast feathers were also used."

Garcia switched to the subject of the birds' natural enemy, black rats that ate their eggs. "Today," he concluded, "many indigenous forest birds are rare, some are extinct, and others are thought to be."

"Like the Kauai 'o'o," Franks commented, "until old Doc here proved them wrong."

Josh had been deep in his own dreary thoughts about his father, but he became alert at the mention of the rare birds now out of sight at the far end of the cave.

He looked at the little poacher. "Eddie told me why he's so

interested in birds, but how come you know so much about them, Mr. Garcia?"

Garcia shrugged, but his partner answered for him. "I'll tell you why. He was studying to be a biologist, but he got greedy."

Garcia scowled at the big man. "I might not have been if I hadn't met you."

"You got no room to complain," Franks said. "You've made a whole lot more money working with me than you ever would have as a state or federal biologist."

Josh nodded, understanding a lot more about Garcia.

"Well," Franks said, shoving himself to his feet and stretching. "I'm going to stretch my legs."

Josh leaped up, fearful that the poacher would walk to the other end of the cave and see the 'o'o birds. He warned, "Don't forget that billy goat over there."

"Oh, yeah. Thanks. I don't want to disturb him."

Again, Josh fought down an urge to laugh. Instead, he said with a straight face, "How about telling us about yourself, Mr. Franks?"

"What's to tell? I make good money giving rich collectors around the world what they want." He started toward the far end of the cave.

Josh stepped in front of him. "Such as?" he prompted.

"What's it to you, kid?" Franks demanded roughly.

"Nothing, except I'm sure you've had an exciting life, doing what you do."

Garcia laughed without humor from behind Josh and Franks.

"He sure has! Poaching rhinos for their horns to sell to the Asian market, machine-gunning elephants for their ivory. . . ."

"Shut up, you fool!" Franks whirled about to face his little partner.

Garcia defiantly thrust out his long neck and said stubbornly, "If I get out of this storm alive, I'm going to give up this business."

"Sure you are, you little cockroach," Franks snapped sarcastically. "You'd starve, trying to do anything else. You would have already, if it hadn't been for me."

"That's enough!" the pilot said sternly.

Franks muttered something under his breath and turned abruptly away. He stepped around Josh and started striding across the cave floor toward the entrance.

The goats stirred uneasily, causing all three birds to flutter into the air at the far end of the cave.

Franks stopped with an oath, then stared hard.

Josh knew the poacher had identified the rare 'o'o birds.

"So," he roared, turning angrily toward the others. "All of you except Garcia knew about those birds, but you've been holding out on me!"

Tank said hoarsely, "Oh-oh!"

Now what? Josh wondered as the big man strode angrily toward him and the others.

Chapter Fourteen

WHEN TIME RUNS OUT

Josh shifted uneasily as Franks moved purposefully toward him and the others, his face twisted into an angry scowl.

"Trying to make a fool out of me, were you?" he thundered. "Trying to keep me from knowing those birds were there! Well, your little secret is out!"

Garcia protested, "Now, Franks, don't go. . . ."

"Shut up!" Franks shoved his partner roughly. "Which one of you decided to keep me from knowing that those birds were in the other end of the cave?" He stopped a few paces in front of the others, hands on his hips, his legs spread, ready to attack. "Speak up!"

The pilot and Eddie started to rise defensively, but Dr. Nakamura spoke first. "You can blame me for that."

"I'm going to blame all of you!" Franks threatened. "I should . . ." his voice trailed off. He added softly, "Well, maybe you've all done me a big favor."

"Don't even think about taking those birds with you," the ornithologist warned.

The big man laughed. "You sure have a suspicious mind,

Dr. Nakamura. But with your bum leg, you couldn't stop Garcia and me if we wanted the birds."

"Maybe he couldn't," the helicopter pilot said evenly. "But I could."

Eddie added, "And I'd be glad to help you, Keegan."

"Now, now!" Franks said with a disarming smile. "There's no need for any of you to get upset. Garcia and I have no plans to take your precious birds."

Josh almost choked at what he knew was a lie, but he was grateful that Franks' anger seemed to have cooled. He eased down against the cave wall and stared toward the far end of the cave. Josh was positive that Franks was planning how to steal the birds.

Gradually the hurricane's fierce winds and horrendous downpour tapered off. With Dr. Nakamura supported between Eddie and the pilot, Josh joined the others in peering out of the mouth of the cave. His heart sank at the utter desolation.

Countless trees had been blown down. Those that still stood had been stripped of leaves and flowers. Below the cave in the flat areas, there was no place for the five hours of drenching rain to run off, so water stood everywhere.

Josh exclaimed, "How will we wade through that?"

"We'll find a way," Eddie said confidently, "but it'll be far worse than what we had coming in. Unless we can follow the high ridges, we'll sink up to our armpits."

Keegan added thoughtfully, "We don't have enough food and water to stay here until the ground dries. We have no choice but to try walking out."

"You able-bodied people can do that," Dr. Nakamura reminded them, gently touching his injured foot, "but I'll have to stay here until you can send a helicopter for me."

Keegan promised, "I'll personally fly back for you as soon as I can. But it's going to be dark shortly, so we'll have to wait here until morning before starting."

After a brief discussion, it was decided that Eddie, his daughter, and their dog would stay with Dr. Nakamura. Keegan would walk out with Josh and Tank, then fly a helicopter back to take the remaining hurricane survivors to safety.

Dr. Nakamura gave his compass to the pilot to help them reach safety.

Josh motioned for Tank to follow him away from the others. "I absolutely *must* find my dad before we leave this area," Josh said desperately.

Tank sighed. "But you don't even know where to start looking."

"Well, we know he left the cave during the eye of the hurricane to get those backpacks. But since Mr. Franks brought one back and saw the other in the river, we know Dad didn't get very far."

"I hate to say this, but what if those two poachers *did* find your dad, and took the backpacks. . .?"

"No!" Josh broke in. "They're poachers, but I don't think they'd do something terrible to anyone."

Tank shrugged. "I hope you're right, but . . ."

"I know!" Josh interrupted. "I won't believe my dad is dead! He's alive, but probably sick or hurt. Otherwise, he'd have come back here."

"I'll help you look for him as soon as it's light enough to see in the morning."

As the hurricane's remnants faded into the distance, the big green frogs hopped out of the cave. The black and brown goats remained until just before darkness fell.

The apapane and 'o'o birds also stayed. Dr. Nakamura explained that they couldn't fly at night. The birds huddled on the ground at the far end of the cave.

Gradually, each person settled down to sleep. Josh planned to do that sitting up, but to keep his ears tuned in to the two poachers. He feared they would try to sneak off with the 'o'o birds.

The cave grew quiet, terribly quiet after the hurricane's furious sounds. Slowly, Josh drifted off to sleep. He dreamed about the argument with his sister.

***

In the darkness under the wrecked house and roof, Nathan asked plaintively, "Will they ever find us?"

Tiffany tried to ignore her painful insides. "Of course they will. I imagine that Mom and Mrs. Nakamura are already trying to get to us from inside the house, but nobody can work outside in this terrible wind. We'll just have to be patient until it stops."

"When will that be?"

"Well, the eye of the hurricane has already passed. We're now in what they call the 'back side' of it and it is supposed to be shorter. So maybe an hour or so more."

"It's already been forever."

"It only seems like it."

The little boy sighed. "I think we're going to die this time."

"No, we're not! Don't even think that!"

"Well, if we do, I'm going to heaven. Will you?"

"Of course," she replied, then choked, remembering the lies she'd told.

"Even after what you said to Josh?"

Tiffany was rattled. "Was that so terrible?"

"We learned in Sunday school that if we don't forgive our brother, God won't forgive us."

"This is different," Tiffany said stiffly, but she was bothered by Nathan's words.

"Besides," he continued, "if your brother has something against you, you're supposed to go to him and make up. Dad read that to us a few days ago. Remember?"

Tiffany didn't reply, but the words burned in her.

***

Josh awakened with a crick in his neck. In the cave's darkness, he rubbed the sharp, piercing spasm and peered around at the others, all of whom were asleep.

No, not everyone, he realized with a start. *Franks and Garcia are gone.*

Silently, Josh got to his feet and hurried to the cave's mouth. He was surprised to see that it was dawn. Low on the horizon, a full moon still rode the sky.

There was light enough to see two sets of fresh footprints in the mud, leading down the hill, away from the cave. Suddenly, Josh remembered something.

The birds! He rushed to the far end of the cave. He almost stepped on the common apapane before realizing it was dead. However, the pair of rare 'o'o's were gone.

Franks and Garcia took them! Josh realized. He roused Tank and the others.

Everyone quickly checked around to see if anything else was missing. Dr. Nakamura's backpack was gone. It had contained what little food there was. The gunnysack that Franks had carried was also missing.

Dr. Nakamura explained, "The poachers undoubtedly used it to carry the birds. They were helpless and couldn't fly because it was too dark for them to see in this cave. They were easy prey for Franks and Garcia."

Tank commented, "I thought Garcia said he wasn't going to have anything more to do with Franks."

Josh was disappointed in the little man, but defended him. "Maybe Mr. Franks forced him to go."

"Could be," Malama admitted. She turned to her father. "Is there any chance we can catch those guys and free the birds?"

Eddie looked doubtful. "They've got a head start, and they know the swamp well. But with all this rainfall, some of the landmarks are going to be hard to find."

"They have a map," Josh said, and quickly told about finding it in the helicopter and losing it back to Franks in the shack.

Dr. Nakamura shook his head. "They must have stolen it early yesterday morning when John and I saw them in our camp. Then they must have headed back to civilization, figuring they could use the map to come back later and trap the birds."

"Well," Keegan observed, "our first priority now is to get safely back to Princeville." He reached into his pocket and pulled out Dr. Nakamura's compass. "We won't get lost with this, so let's go."

Josh, Tank, and the pilot said good-bye to Eddie, Malama, and Dr. Nakamura. The moon had finally set when Josh and Tank trailed Keegan down the slippery hillside.

They followed the poachers' tracks in the first light of day. The tracks headed straight toward the stream that everyone had crossed yesterday, before the deluge.

Josh kept looking in all directions for some sign of his father. Occasionally, he glanced up at the sky. The typical Hawaiian beauty had returned with a few fluffy clouds and gentle trade winds. Only the ground held evidence of Iniki's passage.

From the base of the ridge containing the cave, the flatlands were under water except for some volcanic ridges. Franks' and Garcia's tracks ended at the start of the flooded areas.

Josh glanced apprehensively around, but the poachers were nowhere in sight. There was no sign of Josh's dad.

Keegan commented, "So far, so good. Now we start wading through standing water until we reach the stream. There's been so much rain it might be as wide as the Mississippi River. I just hope we can cross it safely."

Josh followed the man, slogging through warm water filled with floating debris, a dead black rat, and the tips of stunted trees and drowned brush. The mud beneath sucked at the travelers ankles and sometimes to their knees. It was exhausting, slow-going and discouraging. Still, they kept on, with Josh's eyes probing far and near for some place where his father might have found shelter.

A strange silence gripped the swamp. There was no evidence of birds, goats, wild pigs, or feral dogs.

"I haven't heard a bird since we started," Tank commented when they paused in knee-deep water to catch their breath. "Maybe they're all dead."

"I hope not," the pilot replied. "But remember that Dr. Nakamura said some kinds of birds haven't been seen in this place since the last hurricane ten years ago."

Tank exclaimed, "I sure wish we could find those poachers and free those 'o'o birds! Then they could build nests next year and start bringing their kind back from near extinction."

Josh didn't answer, but he felt the same way about wanting the 'o-'o pair freed. Still, he preferred finding his father to ever again seeing Franks or Garcia.

The trio continued on while Josh's hopes for finding his father grew ever dimmer.

The sun rose, making a blinding sheet of light on the flooded flatlands around them. Josh wished for sunglasses, while Keegan periodically checked his borrowed compass.

He led them out of the flooded flatlands and across the base of a small hill. The going was easier now although Josh was miserable with water sloshing in his tennis shoes. After a few moments, the pilot stopped and listened, giving Josh a sudden surge of hope.

"Do you hear somebody?" he asked. "Maybe my father?"

"Sorry, Josh. I hear the stream that we crossed yesterday. It's just around the next bend."

Tank said, "It sure sounds wild. Do you think we can cross it?"

"We'll soon find out." Keegan started walking again.

The survivors went forward while Josh took a last few hopeful looks around for his father. He half-whispered in desperation, "He has to be somewhere close by. But where?"

"Josh," Keegan said gently, turning around and laying a comforting hand on the boy's shoulder. "We've looked every step of the way here. Your father . . ."

"Don't say it!" Josh broke in.

"I hope he's okay," the pilot replied, "but time's running out to find him. Once we cross that stream, the going will be easier and we'll soon be out of the swamp."

Perspiration started trickling down Josh's back as he reached the end of the hill and looked around the bend. He stopped in dismay.

The small stream they had crossed yesterday was out of its banks and running as wild and free as a Mainland river. A few small trees that had survived the wind's fury writhed in the swift-moving, muddy water, while others had been uprooted. They were swept away with the rest of the debris rushing past.

Then Josh saw one lone man standing in hip-deep mud just out of the stream's path. His back was toward Josh, but he could see the man was struggling vainly to free himself from the sucking mud.

"Dad!" Josh shouted, running recklessly off the little hillside.

His voice made the trapped man swivel his head around, and Josh's hopes plunged again. *Mr. Garcia!*

When Josh, Tank, and Keegan got within ten feet of the struggling man, he called a warning. "Don't come any closer, or you'll get stuck too."

"Where's your partner?" the pilot asked.

"Ran off and left me." Garcia swore angrily. "Left me here to die after threatening my life in the cave if I didn't help him steal the birds."

"Where are they?" Josh asked.

"Took them with him. Can you get me out of here?"

Keegan said, "Stand still so you don't sink any deeper. Boys, let's look around for a long branch or something we can use to get him out."

Josh had mixed feelings as he located a broken ohia branch about fifteen feet long. He was sick at heart because he hadn't found his father, but as long as they were trying to rescue Garcia, there was a chance Josh might yet find his father in the area.

Keegan took the branch that Josh dragged up and eased it out over the treacherous mud toward Garcia. He reached out and drew the end toward him. Josh and Tank pulled with the pilot on the other end, but the branch broke, sending Josh, Tank, and Keegan sprawling.

Garcia screamed, "Quick! Find another limb before I sink out of sight in this guck!"

"It's not quicksand," the pilot assured the trapped man.

"Just stop struggling so you won't sink any deeper while we find another branch."

Josh, Tank, and Keegan spread out and searched, but found no branch long enough to reach the victim. Then Josh remembered something.

"There was a rope in that old shack! It's not far, so I'll run get it."

Both Tank and the pilot called a warning to be careful, but Josh barely heard. The trip to the old shack gave him a few more precious moments to look for his father.

As Josh splashed away, his thoughts again flashed to his sister.

Tiffany, Mom, and Nathan should have been a lot safer with Mrs. Nakamura in her house than we were in the cave. So Tiffany and I can talk about . . .

He broke off at his first glimpse of the shack, now a total wreck. The large ohia tree that had stood beside it had crashed into it. There was now only a pile of corrugated metal and broken timbers under the log.

I sure hope I can find the rope in that mess. He stepped on the edge of a twisted piece of corrugated metal sheeting. It clattered noisily.

Suddenly, Josh stopped dead still, listening.

A voice called faintly, "Hello? Is anybody there?"

Chapter Fifteen

A TERRIBLE CHOICE

Josh stood on the rubble of the shack, looking toward the downed ohia tree where he had heard the voice.

"Dad?" The single word carried a world of hope.

"Josh? Is that you?" Mr. Ladd's voice was weak.

"Yes!" Josh shouted with relief. "I'm here, Dad! Where are you?"

"I'm under the fallen tree."

Josh clattered across the corrugated metal toward the downed tree. "I'm coming! Keep talking."

"Okay. I'm sure glad you're here!"

Josh reached the tree and searched quickly through its stripped and bare branches. He fought off a sickening image of what he would see when he reached his father.

Josh called, "Can you hear me?"

"Yes, you're a few feet away."

Josh took a couple of quick steps toward the voice, his eyes probing desperately. "Keep talking, Dad."

"All right. I went to look for some backpacks, but the water was so deep from the hurricane that I was delayed. The eye passed, and I had to take shelter in the shack. After the storm was almost past, I started to leave. Then when the tree fell, wrecked the shack, and trapped me."

Josh, following his father's voice, heard him add, "How'd you get here, son?"

"A helicopter pilot flew me in." Josh didn't say anything about the chopper being forced down. "We found the cave with Dr. Nakamura. He's okay."

"You're right above me now. Shove those branches aside and you should be able to see me."

Wildly, the boy obeyed. Sunlight hit his father's face, making him close his eyes. His face was streaked with rain and dirt. His dark hair was damp on his forehead, he was thoroughly soaked, and was a mass of cuts and bruises. But he was alive.

Josh wanted to shout with joy. Instead, he reached down to touch his father and whispered, "Oh, Dad!"

Mr. Ladd carefully opened his eyes, squinting at the sunshine until Josh thrust his open palm out to cast a shadow over his dad's face. "I'm in a little depression so the weight of the tree isn't on me, but my right arm is trapped, and I can't free it with the other."

"Is it broken?"

"No, thank God. Some branches are between it and a bigger branch so my circulation isn't cut off. I won't lose the arm. But

I can't free myself, and I'm afraid of trying to push the branches away with my feet because the whole tree could move and crush me. Your pilot must be nearby, so please run and get him."

Josh didn't want to waste time explaining that Mr. Keegan was with Tank, trying to save a poacher trapped in deep mud. Josh protested, "I can't leave you!"

"Nothing's going to hurt me now unless this log shifts. I keep passing out from the pain, but once late yesterday when I came to, I saw that a big wild pig had taken shelter under here with me. I guess we were both scared of each other, but more afraid of the hurricane. He left when it passed. Now, please get help."

With a strangled cry, Josh stood. "Okay, Dad. I'll be back as soon as I can."

He turned away and started to run, then remembered Garcia's plight.

The rope! Josh looked around and saw one end under a piece of corrugated metal. He quickly pulled it free, realizing with some alarm that the rope was old and frayed. It might not hold Garcia's weight.

"What are you doing, son?" Mr. Ladd asked anxiously.

"Getting this rope."

"Why do you need that?"

"Tell you later," the boy answered, quickly clutching the rope in both hands. He hurried away as fast as possible in the slippery mud.

His mind raced with the problems now confronting him. He

didn't want to take time to rescue Garcia. But what if the river rose more and drowned him?

And what about Dad? The ground's so soft that the log could shift and crush him. It's too far back to the cave to ask Eddie to help.

Josh determined to let Mr. Keegan decide. Josh coiled the rope as he ran. He slowed as he reached level ground and the stream again came in sight. It seemed even higher and faster than before, moving with such force that small logs, uprooted trees and brush were swept along.

Anyway, once Dad's safe, Josh decided, *I'm staying with him, even if he can't walk and we both have to wait for a helicopter to . . . What's that on the bank?*

At first, it looked like a shapeless brown mass about two feet high. Then Josh recognized it as a burlap bag. It moved slightly.

That's the sack Mr. Franks used to steal the 'o'o birds. They're in it, and alive.

Josh shot concerned glances in all direction, but didn't see the big poacher. Josh shifted the rope to his left hand while running toward the bag. Without slackening his pace, he reached down with his right hand and snatched up the closed top.

"Just a minute, little birds," he said softly as they fluttered in the bottom of the sack. "I'll untie this and you can go free again."

"Hey, kid! Stop that!"

Franks' angry yell startled the boy so much he stopped fumbling with the sack and glanced away from the river. The big poacher stood on the high ground, holding one end of a large ohia log. The other end dragged in the mud. Josh guessed that Franks had set the birds down to find a log to help him cross the river with the rare birds in their sack.

Josh didn't stop. He increased his speed as best he could in the muddy footing. He hitched the coiled rope over his left shoulder, freeing both hands to open the sack.

The birds let out frightened *skree, skree* cries and fluttered their wings against the sack's sides. "Sorry, birds," Josh panted, "but I'm doing the best I can."

"Kid, when I catch you, I'm going to leave you for the wild dogs!" Franks roared.

Josh risked a glance back while his fingers plucked frantically at the top of the sack. The big poacher had dropped the log to run rapidly down the slick hillside toward the fleeing boy.

Can't let him catch me! Josh's wild thought was followed by the realization that he was losing time during which the fallen tree could shift and crush his father. Even carrying the sack of endangered birds slowed him down, and if Franks caught him. . . .

Josh forced the thought away. For one moment, he considered dropping the birds so he could run faster and escape Franks. Then Josh shook his head. *I've almost got it! Another couple of seconds and . . . there!*

The knot in the sack gave way. The top fell open. He instantly turned the bag upside down and shook it.

"Sorry, birds," he apologized as they dropped out, wings

extended to help break their fall. "But that's all I can do for you. Go on! Fly! Get out of here!"

Josh didn't dare stop. He waved his hands as the birds settled to the muddy ground and Franks' mighty yell tore the morning air.

"Now you've done it, kid!"

Josh ran on, slipping and sliding, but clutching the sack so that if the birds couldn't fly and Franks caught them, he'd have no way of keeping them.

Risking another look back, Josh saw with satisfaction that one bird was in flight, heading over the rampaging river. The other still fluttered on the ground as Franks bore down on it.

"Fly, you dumb bird!" Josh shouted, waving his hands so hard the coil of rope slid off his left shoulder.

The 'o'o thrust out its wings and tried to drag itself toward the river, following the direction its companion had taken. But the poacher, with a triumphant cry, reached down with open hands for the bird.

It fluttered mightily, beating its wings so hard it was airborne for a few feet. Josh unconsciously slowed his pace to watch.

Swearing furiously, Franks again grabbed for the bird as it settled just inches from the water's edge.

"Go on, little bird!" Josh cried, feeling a sudden warmness behind his eyes like hot tears forming. "Don't let him catch you again!"

For a moment, Josh thought of running back and giving the big man a shove, but he was too far away. Besides, every moment lost in getting help to his father jeopardized his life.

The poacher's big hands were inches from the bird when it suddenly cried out and launched itself into the air. Straight across the river it flew, wings beating furiously as it tried to keep from falling into the rushing water.

"Go! Go!" Josh called.

He glanced toward Franks just as he slipped and lost his balance. He fell forward, landing with a big splash. Instantly, the powerful current caught him and whirled him away from the shore.

Josh stopped dead still, seeing out of the corner of his eye that the second bird had cleared the far side of the river and was still flying. But Josh's focus was now concentrated on the big poacher.

Franks was swept along so swiftly that he barely let out a strangled cry before he was sucked under. Only his hands remained in sight as the silt-filled river closed over him.

"O, Lord, no!" Josh's startled exclamation was a prayer torn from his heart.

Without thinking, he ran toward the river's edge, not having the faintest idea of how to help the big man. *Where is he? There!*

Franks' head reappeared in the muddy stream. His face was contorted in terror. He thrashed wildly with his hands, grasping at nearby twigs and other small flotsam within reach. "Help!" he screamed.

Josh ran down to the water's edge, but the poacher was too far out. Josh watched helplessly.

Just as Franks started to go under again, he was swept into the crotch of a leafless tree that had stood on dry ground before the hurricane.

For a moment, Josh stood, too scared to think straight about what had just happened. He watched as Franks clutched the tree and hoisted himself up to where he could stand in the tree crotch, clutching the bare limbs with both hands.

"Stay there!" Josh yelled, remembering the rope.

Franks nodded wordlessly, gasping for breath and staring in horror at the surging water below.

Josh dropped his left shoulder so the rope fell into his hands. Then he froze as a fearful thought struck him.

Dad! I'll lose time trying to help Mr. Franks, and that tree could shift and kill my dad.

The boy hesitated, rope in hand, his mind spinning. He knew that he should run on to the pilot and get him to help rescue his father.

Mr. Garcia won't die in the mud, and Mr. Franks is safe in that tree, so Mr. Keegan and I could go rescue Dad and then come back and help these men.

"I'll be back," Josh shouted. He started jogging toward where he'd left the pilot and the little poacher.

"Wait, kid!" Franks' desperate call made Josh turn toward him. He motioned with one hand. "Don't leave me. I can feel the roots of this old tree starting to give way! Throw me that rope before . . ."

He broke off with a frightened yelp as the tree suddenly slipped six inches down toward the water.

Josh slid to a halt and stood with pounding heart and whirling emotions.

If the tree continued to slip, Franks would be thrown back into the water. He might be able to cling to the tree, but suppose it was so waterlogged that it would not float? If Josh took time to help save this man who had given him nothing but trouble, the delay might cost the life of his father.

"Don't stand there, kid!" Franks yelled, his voice high and thin with terror. "Throw me that rope!"

As Josh hesitated, torn between the terrible options facing him, the poacher yelled again.

"This thing's starting to slip again, and I can't swim! Do you hear me? I can't swim!"

Josh moaned as he thought of his father and the consequences of further delay in rescuing him. But if Josh didn't help the poacher, he would surely drown.

Josh knew he had to make the choice, now. He groaned in a silent, anguished prayer. *Lord, what should I do?*

Chapter Sixteen

DESPERATE MOMENTS

Franks shrieked in mortal terror, "I can't swim! Help me!"

Josh thought of his father, buried under the collapsed shack and the downed tree. The boy cast a desperate glance heavenward. *Lord, I can't let Mr. Franks drown, but please keep my dad safe until I can get back to him with some help!*

Josh began rapidly uncoiling the rope. He raised his voice to be heard above the rushing waters. "I'll throw the rope to you. Tie it around your waist. I'll pull you to shore." He grimly added to himself, *I hope.*

He realized that because the poacher was a lot heavier than him, the swift current could pull him into the water to be drowned.

Can't let that happen, Josh thought. *Maybe I can tie my end to that old stump over there. . . .*

"Hurry, kid! This old tree's starting to slip!"

Josh threw the rope with all his strength, but the end fell short. It rapidly floated downstream. Josh hastily began pulling it ashore.

"Hurry, kid! Hurry!"

"Okay, okay!" Josh frantically retrieved the rope. "The end's too light. I've got to tie something on it to make it heavier so it'll travel farther."

He glanced around and found a small branch about a foot long. Keenly aware that his father's life was endangered by each moment's delay, Josh hurriedly tied the wet end of the rope around the center of the stick.

"It'll be your fault if I drown, kid!"

"I'm doing the best I can!" Josh checked the rope to make sure there were no tangles in it. At the same time, he noticed that the strands were badly frayed.

"Don't let me drown!" The poacher's voice cracked with fear. "This tree's slipping real fast!"

Josh didn't waste breath answering. He looked upstream, calculating where to throw the stick so it would drift to where Franks could reach it. Then he heaved the stick with all his strength.

It sailed high into the morning sun, the frayed rope trailing after. Josh watched anxiously as the stick reached the peak of its arc, then fell into the stream. The muddy current caught the stick, carrying it and the rope toward the tree where Franks clung precariously.

Josh held his breath, fearful that the stick would pass just inches beyond the man's reach. Then an eddy caught it, and bore it in a bobbing motion near the tree.

"Grab it!" Josh yelled. Dropping his end of the rope, he shouted through cupped hands. "Grab it before it passes!"

"I'm . . . trying!" Franks leaned dangerously far out, reaching with clawed fingers of his right hand while clinging to the tree with his left. The he let out a triumphant yell. "Got it!"

"Tie it around yourself and I'll pull you to shore!" Josh braced himself just as the rope caught on a snag sticking out of the water. The rope was jerked from his hands. He started to reach for it when he saw that Franks was trying to untie the stick from the other end.

Josh yelled, "Leave the stick on the rope! Just tie it around you, fast!"

The poacher complied, rapidly passed the rope once around his waist and tied it awkwardly.

"Look out!" Josh yelled as the tree suddenly gave way.

It sank with a great splash, breaking Franks' grip. His scream was cut off as he fell heavily into the racing water and sank from sight.

"Mr. Franks!" The boy ran along the bank, watching the swiftly moving water push the tree downstream.

Suddenly, the poacher's head broke the surface, followed by wildly thrashing arms. He sputtered, "Pull me out, kid! Pull. . . ." Water closed over his mouth, breaking off his plea.

The rope! With a startled exclamation, Josh looked down just as the end snaked into the stream.

"No!" Josh screeched, plunging after the rope. The end

seemed to elude his fingers, then they closed over it. *Got it!* Getting a good grip, he turned and waded furiously through the water to the bank. His shoes sloshed as he struggled toward a nearby stump.

"Pull, kid, pull!"

Josh threw two hasty coils of rope around the stump. He tied off the end of the rope just as the last of the slack was taken out by the heavy body on the other end.

The rope leaped from Josh's hands with such force that he was thrown backward. He landed on his seat in the mud.

His eyes darted toward the stream in time to see the rope taut and quivering in the air, throwing silver spray from frayed strands as they popped under the strain.

Josh realized the new danger. *It's going to break.*

He could hear the strands snapping, faster and faster, but there was nothing he could do. If he pulled harder, the rope was sure to snap, and Franks would be lost in the tumbling water.

Suddenly, a whirling eddy formed, propelling Franks toward shore. The line went slack on the surface. Broken strands gave clear visual warning that the rope would not take much more abuse. But Josh had to take that risk.

Hand over hand, he began steadily but rapidly pulling on the weakened rope. *Don't break! Don't break!*

Franks gagged and choked as the eddy eased him toward shore. His eyes were wide with fright as his arms thrashed wildly.

"You're going to make it!" Josh cried, as the man neared the bank. "You're going to . . . oh, no!"

The fickle eddy suddenly whirled about, heading for deep water and carrying the struggling man in its grip.

I'm losing him! The terrifying thought spurred Josh to even faster overhand motions. The rope leaped from the water as it was pulled tight between man and boy.

Franks, obviously seeing the same danger Josh did, began dogpaddling frantically toward shore.

"Look out!" Josh yelled. "The rope broke!"

He watched in horror as the broken end snapped back toward him like a striking snake. Instinctively, he ducked. The broken rope end plopped wetly at his feet.

Josh splashed into the shallow water toward the man. He rolled, helpless as a stick, back toward deep water.

"Grab my hand!" Josh yelled, heedless of his own danger. "Quick, before you're pulled back!"

Franks' big hand closed over the boy's small one. He started backing up in the knee-deep water, but the footing was treacherous.

For a second, Josh lost his balance and thought he was going to be thrown face down into the stream. With a sob of fear and hope, Josh regained his balance, and, with Franks keeping a death grip on his arm, the boy started backing rapidly into shallower water.

Moments later, with most of the poacher's body on shore but his feet still in the stream, both boy and man collapsed, panting hard with fear and exertion.

Dad! Josh's mind flashed back to his father's danger. Even though he was exhausted, Josh struggled weakly to his feet. "I've . . . got . . . to . . ." he panted.

"Relax, Josh, and catch your breath," Franks puffed. "We're safe now."

"But my father's not!" The boy was vaguely aware that the man had used his name instead of calling him by the hated "kid."

Josh bent and struggled to untie the wet rope from around the poacher's waist. "I have to go. A tree fell over on that old shack, and my dad's trapped under it. Oh, and your partner's caught in mud farther downstream. The pilot's trying to help him."

Franks looked behind Josh. "You're wrong about Garcia. Look."

Josh turned to see the little poacher approaching with Tank and Keegan, the helicopter pilot. All three were totally covered with mud.

Garcia called, "Hey, Josh, this pilot is one great guy! He and Tank got another pole and pulled me. . . ."

Josh interrupted. "I'm glad you're all here!" he cried, shoving himself to his feet and quickly explaining about his father's desperate plight.

"Lead the way, Josh!" Keegan exclaimed.

"Thanks!" He turned upstream. Tank, the pilot and Garcia fell in behind him. Josh was aware that Franks had regained his feet, but made no move to follow.

Josh said pointedly, "We could use your help."

"All of you go ahead," Franks replied. "I have to catch my breath."

An angry remark leaped to Josh's lips, but the pilot spoke first.

"Never mind him, Josh. Let's go!"

Josh ran wearily back upstream, recoiling the rope and praying that he wasn't too late.

Josh caught a glimpse of two birds flying overhead. He thought they were the rare 'o'o pair, but couldn't be sure. *I hope they survived,* he thought. *And Mom and Tiffany and Nathan. I wonder how they did in the storm?*

***

A thin shaft of morning sunshine penetrated the cramped wooden prison, striking Tiffany in the face. She moved her face back from the brilliance, but her spirits soared. "Nathan, look! They must be getting closer! I can see sunshine. Move over to where it falls on you so I can check you out."

"I can't." His voice was low and discouraged.

"Sure you can." She reached toward him, but stopped with a stifled moan. Her insides seemed on fire. She gritted her teeth so her little brother wouldn't know how much she hurt.

She knew that Nathan had a head injury, because she had periodically felt the knot on his head. She feared that he had a concussion, but there was no way to be sure.

"Nathan?"

"Huh?" His voice sounded far away.

"I've been thinking, and you were right. I mean, about Josh and me. I realize that I was wrong. I shouldn't have even thought about sneaking out with Rusty. And I shouldn't have argued with Josh. He was just trying to protect his sister."

"Like you did for me when the house fell on us."

Tiffany didn't seem to hear. She added, "And I shouldn't have lied to Mom or Rusty. I'm going to tell Josh how sorry I am for the way I acted toward him." She added to herself, *If I ever get the chance.*

"That's good," Nathan answered wearily. "It's been hours. Do you really think they'll get us out of here?"

"We can still hear them digging, and we answer when they call. They'll get us out as soon as they can."

"I hope so. I'm so . . . tired. So very, very . . ." his voice trailed off.

For several minutes, Tiffany hugged herself tightly, fighting off the waves of nausea that swept her from the pain in her body. With tears of mental and physical agony, she began to pray. It was the first time she'd been able to do that in days.

She didn't know how long she poured out her silent confession, but she felt better when she had finished.

Then she realized that her little brother had been silent a long time. "Nathan? You okay?"

There was no answer. She carefully felt for his wrist, moving her fingers in vain for what she sought. *I can't feel any pulse!*

***

Running toward the spot where he'd left his father, followed by Tank, Keegan, and Garcia, Josh thought momentarily of telling how he had freed the birds, but he saved his breath. He could tell them about that later.

As they neared the collapsed shack and fallen tree again, he called, "Dad, I'm back! I've brought help."

There was no answer.

Josh dashed to the place where he had left his dad and frantically shoved branches aside. "The tree has shifted!" Josh cried to Tank, Keegan and Garcia.

Mr. Ladd's bloody, dirty face was still upturned, but his eyes were closed. Josh tried to shake off the thought that his father had been crushed when the tree moved. "Maybe he passed out!" Josh cried. "Let's get him out, fast!"

"Careful, Josh!" Keegan warned. "Let me see first."

The pilot knelt and carefully examined the situation. "The tree is starting to slip sideways because of the mud. It's too dangerous to work on the downside of the tree, so we'll have to get him out from this side. Everyone, grab something to dig with."

With broken pieces of timber and small segments of corrugated metal, Josh, Tank, Keegan, and Garcia carefully dug away the soft ground. They carved a three-foot-wide segment toward, and then under, the log.

With maddening slowness, they also broke off pieces of branches or bent them aside until they could kneel beside the unconscious victim.

"Now," Keegan said, puffing from exertion, "all of you grab some of those heavier broken timbers from the shack. Let's make a wedge between the branches and his arm."

When that was done, the pilot slowly freed Mr. Ladd's

trapped arm. The pilot motioned for everyone to take hold of Mr. Ladd's shoulders.

"Pull him out gently," Keegan puffed, "and let's hope this tree doesn't slip now."

Josh prayed silently and fervently during the long moments it took to ease his father free of danger. A few minutes later, Mr. Ladd had been half-carried, half-dragged a few feet away from the shack's rubble and gently placed full-length on the wet ground.

Josh cradled his father's head in his arms, moaning softly and whispering, "Oh, Dad, you're safe! Please open your eyes! Please! Please!"

The sun, riding well up in the morning sky, fell across Mr. Ladd's face. His eyes slowly opened.

He said weakly, "Glad . . . glad you're back, son."

Josh hugged his father, his eyes filled with grateful tears.

After a moment, the pilot said softly, "You'd better let me check him over now."

Tank and Garcia led Josh back a few steps while Keegan made a hasty examination, then joined them.

"His arm is broken. He keeps passing out from the pain. Maybe he also has some internal injuries. Josh, he needs a doctor—fast. Garcia, if you'll help the boys make Mr. Ladd as comfortable as possible, I'll hurry back to Princeville for a helicopter. . . ."

"I shouldn't have stopped to help Mr. Franks!" Josh broke in. "I wasted time. . . ."

"Stop it!" the pilot said firmly but gently. "You did the right thing. If you hadn't helped Franks, he would certainly be dead by now. Your father's got a chance if he has medical attention soon." He turned downstream. "I'll be back as fast as possible."

"Be careful," Garcia called after him. Then the little poacher knelt beside the boy and his father. "Keegan's right, Josh. You did the right thing. I'm sure that your father would say the same."

"There were hard choices to make," the boy admitted in a low, pained voice. "The decision had to be made fast. But if I lose Dad. . . ."

"You did all you could. Now it's out of our . . ." He broke off suddenly, then added, "The pilot's saying something, but he's too far away to hear."

Josh looked toward Keegan, who was waving both hands over his head and jumping up and down like a wild person. "What in the world. . . ?" Josh muttered, then broke off his thought as sunlight reflected off of something approaching in the sky.

"Helicopter! It's coming this way!"

Moments later, as Keegan raced, slipping and sliding back toward the wrecked shack, a brightly painted Rainbow Helicopter slowly eased down above the survivors.

Chapter Seventeen

FRANTIC RESCUE EFFORTS

There was no place to land, but that didn't matter. The chopper hovered a few feet off the ground, but far enough from the wrecked shack that the overhead rotary blast wouldn't throw pieces of the debris and injure anyone. Josh, Tank, Keegan, and Garcia helped Mr. Ladd to his feet.

He regained consciousness and was able to walk, supported between Keegan and Garcia, to where he could be hoisted into the helicopter.

Josh buckled his father into the back seat, then sat beside him. Tank and Garcia sat in the middle. Keegan moved up front beside the rescue pilot.

As the helicopter climbed high into the morning sky, Josh raised his voice to be heard above the engine noise. He introduced his dad to Keegan and Garcia, and told how they and Tank had helped pull him from under the tree.

Mr. Ladd thanked them all, then smiled wanly at Garcia. "I guess it's just as well that Dr. Nakamura and I didn't catch you and your partner when we chased you out of our camp early yesterday morning."

The little poacher smiled. "I'm glad you didn't."

Josh asked, "How do you feel, Dad?"

"My arm hurts, but I don't think there's anything else seriously wrong with me. In fact, now that I'm out from under that tree, I feel better every minute. But I'm really concerned about your mother, sister, and brother."

Josh swallowed hard. "So am I."

***

At that moment, under the wreckage where rescuers had been clawing all through the night and into the morning, Tiffany fought back a scream.

I can't feel Nathan's pulse! I can't . . . She felt him stir under her fingers. "Oh, Nathan!" she sobbed, bending over him. "I thought you were . . ." She broke off upon hearing her mother's voice. She seemed to be calling from a great distance.

"We're here, Mom! Under here!" Tiffany picked up a piece of wood with which she had periodically pounded at their tiny prison. "Here! Here! Oh, please hurry!" She thumped in frustration against the shattered shell that encased them.

Nathan sighed. "I'm so . . . tired."

"It won't be long now! Hang on! Hang on!"

The little boy didn't answer. Tiffany anguished silently, *Did he survive the hurricane only to die now? Time's running out—fast!* She drove the thought away, but her mind jumped again. *What about Josh? And Dad and the others?*

A terrible stillness seeped over her and Nathan.

***

In the helicopter Keegan spoke to the pilot, then turned and put on a headset while motioning for the other passengers to do the same.

When they had done so, the rescue pilot spoke into his microphone. "My name is O'Brien. Welcome aboard one of the few helicopters on Kauai that survived Iniki."

For the first time since climbing into the chopper, Josh took a good look at the rescue pilot. He was about forty, with reddish hair showing under his headset.

"Mr. O'Brien," Josh's father replied, raising his voice to be heard above the engine noise, "we're the Ladd family. My wife, daughter and younger son were visiting with friends named Nakamura on Kauai. Any chance you've heard from any of them?"

"No, I'm sorry. The phones are all down. In fact, almost everything is down. You'll see for yourself in a few minutes when we fly over them."

O'Brien explained that he and Keegan had flown helicopters together in Vietnam before working together at Rainbow Helicopters. When Keegan radioed yesterday morning that he was taking two boys and two men on an impromptu search mission toward Alakai Swamp, everyone at the heli-copter company had been deeply concerned.

"Then," O'Brien concluded, "after we lost contact and knew Keegan was down, we naturally wanted to search for him and his passengers. However, with the hurricane bearing down, that wasn't possible until this morning. A few minutes ago when I spotted what was left of your chopper, I was afraid I wouldn't find anybody alive. But I flew on, hoping, and found you."

Mr. Ladd said emphatically, "You got here just in time, too! But there still are some other people in a cave back in the swamp."

"Yes, Keegan told me. As soon as we get you folks safely on the ground, we're heading back for them."

Garcia leaned forward in his seat. "There's also another man out there named Franks. Big fellow. He's in the open, alone. Will you watch for him, too?"

"Sure will."

Mr. Ladd asked, "When we land, can I rent a car. . .?"

"Not a chance," O'Brien broke in. "The streets in every com-munity are impassable. In addition to downed trees, wrecked cars, and pieces of houses, wires are scattered everywhere.

"There's no electricity, and there may not be for days or weeks. We get news on battery-operated radios receiving sig-nals from our local radio stations. They're running on genera-tors. We also get information from Honolulu radio stations, where they do have electric power."

Mr. Ladd asked, "Could you set us down somewhere near the

Nakamuras' house? I think I can recognize the neighborhood from up here. I'm desperate to see how my family is doing."

"Well, regulations won't permit me to land in a residential neighborhood, yet in this emergency situation, I'll risk getting you as close as possible."

A terrible question nagged at Josh. He didn't want to ask, but he had to know. "Did anybody . . . die?"

O'Brien nodded. "Unfortunately, at least two people are known dead. Let's hope there aren't any more."

Josh still anguished over the fact that he and his sister had parted with unresolved anger between them.

If she's dead, or Mom, or Nathan . . . Josh shook his head hard to rid himself of the thought.

His father tried to sound reassuring. "I'm sure they'll be all right." He turned to the pilot. "Tell us more about the hurricane."

Josh suspected his father deliberately asked that to shift thoughts away from what might have happened to the Ladd family.

O'Brien's voice again came through Josh's earphones. "Winds were clocked as high as 225 miles an hour. In a minute, you can see for yourself."

Looking out the helicopter's plexiglass window, Josh first glimpsed the Pacific Ocean in the distance. O'Brien said that yesterday it had looked as if it were on fire because the wind-whipped waves resembled smoke.

As the helicopter descended, approaching Lihue, Josh shook his head in amazement. The Garden Isle's beauty had been ravished. Fronds had been so severely battered that they hung like broken feathers from the coconut palm trees. Stately Norfolk pines and ironwood trees sprawled on the ground. Others that Josh couldn't identify rested their uprooted trunks awkwardly across each other like football players after a mass tackle.

O'Brien said that 14,000 buildings on the island were partially or totally destroyed. One out of every three families was homeless.

Looking down from the sky, Josh confirmed the destruction. Roofs were gone from rows of once fine homes. Other houses were flattened, totally ruined. Great boulders had been thrown up from the sea to rest near what was left of a posh beach-front hotel. A pointed steeple lay a hundred yards from the remains of a white frame church.

Finally, Josh's father called, "Mr. O'Brien, this is the right neighborhood. I think that's the Nakamuras' house. . . ."

He left his sentence unfinished while Josh recoiled at the sight below. People were tearing frantically at a roof that had smashed into the Nakamura home.

"Mr. O'Brien!" Josh's father cried. "That's the right house, but something terrible has happened to it."

"I see it. I'll get you as close as possible."

Josh watched in rising fear as the rescuers worked frantically below. *Who's under there?* he wondered.

The chopper descended toward a nearby vacant lot where only the foundation of a house remained. When the aircraft hovered a few feet above the earth, Josh, his father, and Tank swung out the door and onto the ground.

Josh and Tank followed Mr. Ladd, who ran awkwardly,

clutching his injured arm. They dodged around crumpled cars and uprooted plumeria trees, then leaped over palm fronds, heading for the Nakamura home 200 yards away.

As the helicopter rose into the air, some people at the Nakamura home watched the approaching man and boys, but most others continued pulling aside debris. It was obvious to Josh that the full roof from a neighbor's house had violently smashed into the Nakamuras'.

There were no policemen present, and no firemen. The people Josh saw were clearly neighbors desperately digging with their hands and a few small tools at what might be a hurricane-made tomb.

"Do you see your mother or the kids?" Mr. Ladd panted.

Josh scanned the cluster of rescuers. "No," he answered, his mouth dry with fear. "I don't see . . . wait! There's Mom! And Mrs. Nakamura!"

The two women broke from the other rescuers and hurried toward the new arrivals.

"Dad, where's Tiffany?" Josh asked, starting to puff hard from the run. "And Nathan?"

His father didn't answer.

But Josh suddenly knew. *They're under that wreckage!*

Seconds later, with outstretched arms and tears running down her face, Josh's mother collapsed against her husband's chest. "John! Josh! And Tank! Thank God you're all safe!" She reached out with one hand and pulled all three to her. "But Tiffany and Nathan . . ." She couldn't finish, but turned toward the wreckage.

Mrs. Nakamura explained quietly, "A neighbor's roof smashed into our house late yesterday, trapping them."

"Oh, Lord, no!" their father breathed, staring at the debris.

"Are they . . . alive?" Josh blurted.

Mrs. Nakamura replied, "Workmen heard them until a while ago, but . . . " she broke off, then asked, "Where's my husband?"

"Safe in a cave. The helicopter that you saw is heading back for him and some others."

Mrs. Nakamura's eyes filled with tears, and she turned away, her body shaking.

Josh's father gently freed himself from his wife's arms. "Son, you and Tank take care of your mother and Mrs. Nakamura. I've got to help over there."

"I'll go with you, Dad. Your arm . . ."

His father interrupted. "I'll be all right, but your mother and Mrs. Nakamura need you here." He sprinted toward the wreckage, clutching his injured arm.

"Oh, Josh! Josh!" his mother whispered brokenly, pulling him close and hugging him hard. "I'm so glad you're both safe, but we don't know about your brother and sister. . . " she ended in broken sobs.

"They'll be okay," Josh said, freeing one arm to put it around Mrs. Nakamura. But he wasn't at all sure of that as he again looked at the wreckage.

Two women came from the spectators at the wreckage. They put their arms around Mrs. Nakamura and led her away.

Josh called softly after her. "Your husband should be here soon." Josh didn't tell about Dr. Nakamura's injured leg.

Mrs. Nakamura turned to face him, her eyes bright with tears. "I am most grateful," she said with a trembling voice. "Mahalo.*"

Josh nodded as his mother brushed at her eyes with the back of her hand. She briefly recounted details of the accident that had trapped two of her children.

She concluded, "Naturally, it was impossible to go outside in that wind. Mrs. Nakamura and I from inside the house tried to get to them right away, using only our bare hands. When the storm ended, we ran outside. People came with tools and worked right through the night with flashlights, until now."

Josh said quickly, "Mrs. Nakamura said Tiffany and Nathan could be heard until about an hour ago. What about since then?"

"Nothing," Mrs. Ladd said brokenly. "Not a sound."

It's too late! The thought exploded painfully in Josh's mind. The last angry words between himself and his sister echoed in memory. With a shudder, he dropped his head on his mother's shoulder and hugged her hard, tears in his eyes.

He was vaguely aware that she was patting him as she had when he was a little boy.

Suddenly, there was a shout from the wreckage. Josh felt his mother stiffen as he raised his head.

A man in a torn and dirty tee shirt waved his orange hard hat in the air. "We find dem!" he called in the pidgin English* that some locals used. "Both dem 'live, yeah!"

***

Later, in the hospital, Josh sat on the edge of his little brother's bed. Nathan had not suffered a concussion, and he was recovering nicely. Josh finished telling Nathan how he and their father had survived the hurricane, and how Dr. Nakamura, Eddie, Malama, and their dog had also been rescued. Mr. Garcia had given up poaching and was trying to find work in Honolulu. So far, his former partner, Mr. Franks, had not been located.

Nathan told Josh how he and Tiffany had survived under the wreckage. "I cried so hard that I got sleepy," the little boy confessed.

"You scared your sister plenty, doing that," Josh said. "She thought you were dead."

"She thought you were too. She told me something, but I'm not supposed to tell. She wants to do that."

Josh nodded, then explained to Nathan that the doctors said Tiffany had internal injuries as well as numerous scrapes and cuts. Josh had not been allowed to see her until now. Only their parents had been permitted that privilege.

Josh stood when their parents entered Nathan's room. "Your sister's going to be all right," Mr. Ladd said. "She wants to see you alone. The doctor says you may go in now."

When Josh entered her room, she turned her head on the hospital bed and smiled at him.

"Hi," she said weakly, reaching out her hand to him.

He took it. "Hi, yourself."

"I'm sorry, Josh."

"It wasn't your fault. The hurricane just blew that roof right into . . ."

She stopped him with a brief motion of her free hand. "Not that. I'm sorry about . . . our quarrel."

"I'm sorry too."

"It really was my fault, Josh. I was wrong about Rusty. Thanks for trying to make me see that. I even lied to Mom about that, but I just now told her the truth.

"What bothered me most was being under that wrecked house and thinking that I was never going to get to tell you how sorry I was about our quarrel."

"And I was afraid of the same thing because I realized in the hurricane that I should have tried to patch things up right away. Will you forgive me?"

She nodded. "Yes. Forgive me, too?"

He squeezed her hand. "Of course. Oh, one thing more. Let's promise that if we do quarrel, we won't ever again let the day end without making up. Okay?"

" 'Don't let the sun go down on your anger.' That's in the Bible. So, I promise."

"Me, too. Now, you rest easy. Soon we'll all be safely home again in Honolulu."

Tiffany managed a little smile and closed her eyes. Josh walked to the window and looked out toward the west. Beautiful white cumulus clouds over the mountains reflected the setting sun.

But this time it was all right, for it did not set on angry words.

With God's help, it would always be that way.

GLOSSARY

CHAPTER 1

Kauai: (Kuh-wye) An Hawaiian island northwest of Oahu (where Honolulu is located.) Kauai is thought by many to be the most photogenic of the islands.

Na Pali: (nah-polly) The cliff, as in the spectacular Na Pali Coast State Park on Kauai's northwest shore.

Aloha shirt: (ah-LOW-hah) A loose-fitting man's Hawaiian shirt worn outside the pants. The garment is usually very colorful.

Alakai Swamp: (ah-lah-kye) A little known area in the center of Kauai where some of the world's most rare and unique birds and insects live in remote isolation.

Mount Waialeale: (why-ah-lay-ah-lay) The 5,148-foot-high mountain and extinct volcano that created the island of Kauai. It is the world's wettest spot, receiving between 500 and 600 inches of rain annually.

Ornithologist: (or-ne-THOL-oh-gist) A person specializing in the study of birds.

'O'o'a'a: (oh-oh-ah-ah) A very rare Hawaiian bird of the Alakai Swamp forests. It is mostly black in color except for a few tufts of yellow leg feathers. These were highly prized by ancient Hawaiians in their father work.

Princeville: A small community on Kauai's north shore where some sight-seeing helicopters are stationed.

CHAPTER 2

Lihue: (Lee-hoo-ee): A principal city on Kauai's southeast side.

Honolulu: (hoe-no-LOO-LOO) Hawaii's capital and the most populous city in the 50th state is located on the island of Oahu. In Hawaiian, Honolulu means sheltered bay.

Iniki: (ee-nee-kee) Hawaiian for sharp and piercing, as a wind or pangs of love. Used as a proper noun when referring to Hurricane Iniki, the most devastating storm to hit Kauai in a century.

Iwa: (ee-vah) The name given to a Category One hurricane that hit Kauai in 1982.

Lanai: (LAH-nye) Hawaiian for a patio, porch or balcony. Also, when capitalized, Lanai is a smaller Hawaiian island.

Plumeria: (ploo-MARE-ee-yah) Also called frangipani (FRAN-gee-PAN-ee). A shrub or small tree which produces large, very fragrant blossoms. They are popular in leis.

CHAPTER 3

Bougainvillea: (boo-gun-VEEL-ee-yah) A common tropical ornamental climbing vine with small flowers of many colors, including red, lavender, coral, and white.

Hibiscus: (hi-BIS-cus) A common Hawaiian plant having a large, open blossom. Although available in many colors, no particular one is designated for this, the state flower.

Mango: (man-GO) A yellowish-red tropical fruit and the evergreen tree that bears it.

CHAPTER 4

Botonist: An expert in the study of plants.

Feral: (fher-l) Not domesticated, as an animal that has returned to the wild or is descended from tame ancestors.

Poi dog: (poy) An Hawaiian term used for a mongrel or mixed breed dog.

Ohia lehua: (oh-hee-ah lay-hoo-ah) An abundant native Hawaiian tree with colorful, petal-less red flowers that provide nectar for many birds. Some ohias are small, but in certain areas may grow up to 100 feet tall.

O'lapalapa: (oh-lah-pah-lah-pah). An Hawaiian tree on Kauai somewhat in appearance like an aspen with leaves that flutter in the wind. However, the o'lapalapa does not have the aspen's white trunk.

CHAPTER 5

Kahu: (kah-hoo) Hawaiian for guardian.

Hapahaole: (HAH-pah-HOW-lee) Hapa means half or part, so this is a person who's part Caucasian or white, and part nonwhite, as Hawaiian.

Caucasian: (kah-kay-zhon) A person of the white race.

Aloha: (ah-LOW-ha) A versatile Hawaiian word meaning hello, goodbye and love. As used in this story, it is a greeting: hello.

Miha: (mee-hah) Literally, Hawaiian for quiet or flowing. In this book, it is used as a surname.

Malama: (mah-lah-ma) Hawaiian for light or torch.

CHAPTER 7

Waikiki: (why-kee-kee) Hawaii's most famous white sand beach. Waikiki is Hawaiian for Spouting Water.

CHAPTER 8

Haole: (HOW-lee) An Hawaiian word originally meaning stranger, but now used to mean Caucasians, or white people.

CHAPTER 9

Occult: (oh-kult) From the Latin meaning secret or covered, but now commonly used to indicate the mysterious, supernatural, or magic.

CHAPTER 12

Apapane: (ah-pah-pah-nay) An endemic Hawaiian bird with crimson feathers on breast and head, still abundant in native forests of the main Hawaiian islands except Lanai. Feathers were sometimes used in old Hawaiian capes and helmets.